Have you read all th[e]

Book 1
Alice-Miranda
at School

Book 4
Alice-Miranda
at Sea

Book 5
Alice-Miranda
in New York

Book 6
Alice-Miranda
Shows the Way

Book 7
Alice-Miranda
in Paris

Book 8
Alice-Miranda
Shines Bright

The Queen's Cup was the only trophy missing from a cabinet laden with plates and cups and all manner of prizes earned during Evelyn's stellar racehorse training career. She had promised herself that once it was there, she could give up the early morning starts and find a little place to retire. Perhaps she'd do some travelling, buy a few animals to keep the grass down and maybe even write that novel that had been buzzing around in her head forever. Part of her would hate to leave it all – Dick and the lads, Her Majesty and, more importantly, her horses – but she wondered if there was another life out there, waiting to be enjoyed. It was true that she and Dick had a wonderful partnership and there were times when she wished it had grown into something more than just that of trainer and foreman, but she supposed it wasn't to be.

Evelyn patted the horse's neck. 'I think we should be heading out. The Queen's Cup is in three weeks and you won't win it by standing around here all morning.'

She turned and walked towards the tack room to retrieve Rockstar's bridle and the tiny racing saddle she had used since she was a young woman just starting out as a strapper. Evelyn flicked the light switch. Nothing.

'Oh, blast,' she cursed to no one in particular as she walked into the dark room. 'I thought you were having that looked at, Dick Wigglesworth. Oh, what's that?'

There was a sickening thud followed by an ear-piercing whinny that punched a hole in the silence shrouding the stables.

Evelyn Pepper lay in a crumpled heap, uncon-scious, on the floor.

Chapter 1

At Winchesterfield-Downsfordvale Academy for Proper Young Ladies, the dining room hummed with chatter as the girls ate their breakfast and talked about the day ahead. Mrs Smith had made a particularly delicious spread.

'Do the Americans really eat bacon with their pancakes?' Millie asked as she eyed the two crispy rashers sitting alongside the fluffy stack on her plate.

'Oh, yes,' Alice-Miranda replied. 'I first tried it like that when Mummy and Daddy took me to this amazing cafe down on Broadway where all the waiters sing and dance. It's called Ellen's Stardust Diner and it's very famous. Trust me, once you've had the pancakes and maple syrup together with the bacon, you'll never go back.'

Millie shrugged. 'I'm game.'

'It's good that Mrs Smith's trying new recipes,' said Jacinta, 'but I thought it must have been a special day or something. We usually get the really fancy stuff on the weekends.' She loaded her fork and took a mouthful of food. Then Jacinta looked across the table and winked at Millie, who tried to smother a grin.

'Why are you two pulling faces?' Alice-Miranda asked.

'No reason,' Millie and Jacinta said in unison. They giggled conspiratorially.

Alice-Miranda had recently returned from a month in New York City with her parents. While she was away, Miss Grimm had allowed Millie and Jacinta to share a room. The two girls had got on well most of the time but they were both glad when Alice-Miranda arrived home. Jacinta's promise not to leave her dirty underwear lying about had lasted less than a week, and although Millie had tried to bite her tongue, she couldn't help telling Jacinta what she really thought every now and then.

Millie had packed her things and moved back into their old room before Alice-Miranda's plane had touched down on the tarmac.

Jacinta now had a new room mate of her own. Except that she wasn't exactly new.

Alice-Miranda looked up as a tall blonde girl approached the table. 'Hello Sloane, would you like to sit with us?'

'Sure,' the older girl nodded.

Millie and Jacinta both glanced up and said hello.

A lot of girls at school were still wary of Sloane. During her first stay at Winchesterfield-Downsford-vale she had behaved horridly and had helped her mother bring Fayle School for Boys to its knees. But Alice-Miranda, Millie and Jacinta had seen a different side to her. During a cruise on board the *Octavia*, Alice-Miranda had sought Sloane's assist-ance. Sloane had been having such an awful time at her new school that she decided to find out what it would feel like to help someone – not because there was anything in it for her, but just because they had asked. When she had arrived unexpectedly on board the *Octavia* she had been a welcome sight indeed.

Afterwards, Sloane had begged her father to send her back to Winchesterfield-Downsfordvale. A good word from Alice-Miranda and her parents had helped convince Miss Grimm that the girl deserved a second chance. She was currently 'on trial' for the rest of the term and so far had been a model student, much to the surprise of many – especially their housemistress, Mrs Howard. Sloane had even been visiting her step-granny Henrietta at Caledonia Manor on a regular basis. The two of them had struck up a lovely friend-ship and Sloane was surprised to realise that she actually quite enjoyed the old woman's company.

'Doesn't Miss Grimm look lovely today?' Alice-Miranda said as the headmistress, in a striking white suit, moved to the podium beside the teacher's table.

'Good morning, girls. I have some important announcements before you head off to class. I'm sure that you are aware that the Winchesterfield Show, culminating with the running of the Queen's Cup, is coming up in a couple of weeks' time. I know that in the past, I have been somewhat reluctant to allow girls to attend . . .'

'Reluctant! That's an understatement,' Jacinta said behind her hand. 'We've never been allowed to go. Ever!'

Ophelia Grimm glared at Jacinta. 'Is there something you'd like to share with the rest of us, Miss Headlington-Bear?'

Jacinta shook her head and gulped. 'No, Miss Grimm.'

'Well then, I will continue if I may?' The headmistress's left eyebrow arched menacingly. 'I've been speaking with Professor Winterbottom over at Fayle and, in honour of this being the show's 150th continuous year, we are declaring Friday in a fortnight's time a show-day holiday.'

A cheer went up around the room.

'Settle down, girls,' Miss Grimm commanded. 'I am looking forward to seeing all of you entering as many of the events as possible. As today is Monday, you will have less than three weeks to prepare. On the Saturday evening we will all be attending the show ball, and then on Sunday we will come together to enjoy the glamour and fun of the Queen's Cup Carnival – a fitting end to a fabulous weekend, I should think. But we also need lots of helpers. Mrs Smith is going to run the tea rooms for the Village Women's Association and is rather keen for girls to assist. And I know Mr Charles is putting together a plant and flower market and will need some willing workers, too. There will be some sign-up sheets here in the dining room at lunchtime today,' explained Miss Grimm, with a smile at the assembly.

'We'd better do some proper training then,' Millie whispered to Alice-Miranda. 'Do you want to enter all the pairs events?'

Alice-Miranda nodded.

'What pairs?' Jacinta asked. She pulled a face as she registered what the girls were talking about. 'Oh, you mean the stupid horse show. I was just looking forward to the carnival rides.'

'Yeah, me too,' said Sloane.

'You have until next Monday to get your entries to Mrs Derby. I understand there will be a list posted on the noticeboard by this afternoon,' Miss Grimm added, before stepping back from the microphone.

Alice-Miranda looked up at the large clock on the wall. 'Oh! I'd better go. I said I'd help Miss Wall get the hockey kits ready for our PE lesson.' She stood up.

'Excuse me, young lady, where do you think you're going?' Miss Grimm moved back towards the microphone and stared at the tiny child.

'I'm sorry, Miss Grimm. I thought you'd finished the morning announcements. I told Miss Wall that I would help her before class.'

The headmistress was stern. 'I don't think so, Alice-Miranda. You need to sit right back down where you were.'

Alice-Miranda's tummy fluttered. Miss Grimm had changed so much for the better over the past months but right now she seemed a little bit like her forbidding old self again.

Millie, Jacinta and Sloane tried to suppress smiles.

'Surely you didn't think you'd get away with it?' Miss Grimm stared at Alice-Miranda intently.

'I'm sorry, Miss Grimm, but I don't understand what you mean,' she replied.

'Please come up here, Alice-Miranda.'

The child made her way to the front of the dining room and stood on the floor below the podium.

'Danika, Mrs Smith, Miss Reedy, would you like to come in now?' The headmistress turned to her left and beckoned to the head prefect, the cook and the English teacher. 'Haaa–' Ophelia held the note for several seconds. '–ppy birthday to you, happy birthday to you . . .'

The whole room joined in the rousing chorus. Danika entered the room carrying the most beautiful garland of daisies and irises in white and purple, which she placed ceremoniously onto Alice-Miranda's head. Her chocolate curls cascaded beneath the flowery headpiece. Miss Reedy was carrying a beautifully wrapped pink parcel with a huge purple bow and a poster-sized card.

Mrs Smith walked behind Danika and Miss Reedy pushing a trolley loaded with the most enormous chocolate cake, on top of which flickered eight candles.

She stopped in front of Alice-Miranda, who leaned forward on her tippy-toes to blow them out.

'Hip, hip –' Miss Grimm began.

'Hooray!' the girls and teachers replied.

'Hip, hip –'

'Hooray!'

'Hip, hip –'

'Hooray!'

Alice-Miranda's smile lit up the room as she cut the cake.

'Thank you so much, everyone. This is wonderful,' she exclaimed, then rushed over to Mrs Smith and gave her a hug, then onto the podium to

Miss Grimm, who scooped her up and gave her a hug right back.

'You didn't really think we'd forget your birthday?' asked Miss Grimm.

'No. But when nobody said anything this morning, I thought it would be rude to make a fuss. Thank you, Miss Grimm. This is going to be the best birthday ever.' Alice-Miranda hugged the headmistress tightly.

Ophelia deposited the child back to the floor.

'Are you going to open your gift?' Miss Reedy asked.

'It's so beautiful. I think I'd just like to look at it for a while,' Alice-Miranda replied.

'Come on, Alice-Miranda, open it,' Millie called.

'Open, open, open,' the girls chanted.

Alice-Miranda carefully picked at the sticky tape.

'Oh, please!' Jacinta exclaimed. 'We'll be here until lunchtime if you unwrap it like that.'

Alice-Miranda tore open the end of the parcel and pulled out a black velvet riding cap.

'It's lovely,' she said. 'Thank you so much! I'm going to read the card later – it might take me a while.' On the cover was a drawing. It showed everyone at the school with Winchesterfield Manor in the background.

'Susannah made the card,' Miss Reedy told her. 'She's very clever, isn't she?

Alice-Miranda smiled as she noticed herself in the middle of the picture.

'I'm afraid, girls, that while chocolate cake for breakfast does sound strangely appealing, I think we'll save this scrumptious confection for morning tea,' Miss Grimm announced.

A groan rang out around the room.

'Or perhaps you'd rather that the teachers have it for themselves,' the headmistress said with a smirk.

The room fell silent.

'It's time for class. I think Miss Wall might let you off the hook this morning, Alice-Miranda.' The headmistress looked at the PE teacher, who nodded and smiled.

'Thank you, Miss Grimm, that was the best surprise ever,' Alice-Miranda declared.

'You have a lovely day, sweetheart,' Ophelia Grimm replied.

Alice-Miranda waved to Millie, Jacinta and Sloane, who were all grinning from ear to ear, thrilled that their plotting had worked so well.

'See you later,' she called.

'Bye,' the girls chorused. 'See you at morning tea.'

And with that Alice-Miranda skipped out the door.

Chapter 2

The morning flew by. Alice-Miranda had PE followed by Science with Mr Plumpton.

At morning tea time she ran to the dining room where she was greeted by the school secretary, Mrs Derby, holding a beautifully wrapped parcel.

'Hello there. Happy birthday, sweetheart,' the young woman said.

'Thank you, Mrs Derby.' Alice-Miranda gave her a quick hug.

'This arrived for you a little while ago.' Louella

Derby handed Alice-Miranda the gift. It was wrapped in the prettiest striped cerise paper with a huge polka dot bow. Alice-Miranda wondered what was inside.

'There's a card, too,' Mrs Derby pointed out.

Alice-Miranda slid her finger under the flap and opened the envelope. Inside was a gorgeous card with a pony on the front that looked just like Bonaparte. He was baring his teeth and had a speech bubble that said, 'I hear it's your birthday, so I'll try to be on my best behaviour, just this once . . .' On closer inspection Alice-Miranda realised that it *was* Bonaparte. Her mother must have had it specially made.

To our darling daughter,

Wishing you the happiest of birthdays. We can hardly believe that you're as grown up as eight. Have a wonderful day with all your friends and we will see you very soon.

All our love and hugs and kisses,
Mummy and Daddy and everyone at home xoxox

Millie and Jacinta rushed into the dining room and stood beside their friend.

'Did you think we'd forgotten?' Millie gasped as she tried to catch her breath.

'No. Well, not really,' Alice-Miranda replied. 'I thought you might have been playing a trick on me when I saw Jacinta wink at you at breakfast.'

'Hurry up,' Millie ordered, nodding at the parcel. 'Aren't you going to open it?'

Alice-Miranda tore open the paper and pulled out a beautiful silver photo frame.

'Look!' she exclaimed. 'This picture was taken on the *Octavia* at Aunt Charlotte and Uncle Lawrence's wedding – everyone's there.'

'Let me see.' Sloane had arrived and joined the group. 'Look! That's me.' She pointed at herself standing beside Millie.

'Der.' Millie rolled her eyes.

Sloane wrinkled her nose.

'What else is in there?' Jacinta asked.

Alice-Miranda peered into the package and pulled out a beautiful pair of leather riding gloves, several pretty hairclips and a lovely blue dress.

'I've had some other parcels delivered to the house, too,' Mrs Derby said.

Alice-Miranda beamed. 'It sounds like my whole day is going to be full of surprises.'

'Come on,' Millie urged. 'I'm starving and that cake of yours looks really good.' She eyed off the large wedges of chocolate cake set out along the servery.

As the girls ate their delicious morning tea, Millie and Alice-Miranda agreed to meet at the stables at lunchtime and see how Chops and Bony were getting on.

Jacinta said that she was heading off to the gym during the lunch break and Sloane mentioned that she needed to go to the library and make a start on some research for an assignment.

Jacinta stared at her room mate and frowned. 'Who are you and what have you done with the real Sloane Sykes?'

'Jacinta! I think it's wonderful that Sloane wants to get her work done,' Alice-Miranda said.

'Well, I'd rather go to the library than to the stables any day. I'm never riding again – horses are horrible.' Sloane curled her top lip, recalling her last outing on Stumps, which saw her galloping through the woods, completely out of control.

'You know, maybe you're not so bad after all,' Jacinta said and raised her hand to high-five Sloane across the table. 'We might have more in common that I first thought.'

The girls went off to their lessons, and on the way Alice-Miranda ducked into the kitchen to see if she could organise some sandwiches for her and Millie to take with them at lunch.

'Hello, Mrs Smith, are you here?' the child called as she entered the cavernous space. It was filled with rows of stainless steel benches and pots of all shapes and sizes hung overhead like a colony of metal bats.

Doreen Smith was in the coolroom, checking on supplies.

'Wait there a tick, darling girl. I'll be out in a moment,' she called back.

Alice-Miranda stood beside the area of bench that Mrs Smith liked to call her 'office'. There was a corkboard with recipes and a couple of her favourite photographs, including one of Mrs Smith and her good friend Dolly Oliver at Highton Hall, and another of her grandchildren standing in front of the entrance to Disneyland.

'Well, hello there,' the cook said as she emerged from the coolroom.

'Thank you for my scrumptious cake – and that delicious breakfast. I was a bit surprised to find the crispy bacon with the pancakes,' said Alice-Miranda.

'It was my pleasure,' Mrs Smith replied. 'You know I developed quite a taste for that myself when I last visited the grandchildren.'

They were interrupted by the telephone ringing.

'Hang on a tick, dear. I'll just get that,' said the cook as she picked it up. 'Hello Dick, how are you? Really? Oh heavens.' Mrs Smith inhaled sharply. 'Is she going to be all right? What a terrible shock. Just let me know what I can do.' There was a short pause. 'Oh, that's easy, no trouble at all.'

'Is something the matter?' Alice-Miranda asked as Mrs Smith placed the phone back in its cradle and sat down on the stool. Her shoulders slumped as if someone had just pricked her with a pin and all the air was leaking out.

'That was Dick Wigglesworth, the stable foreman at Chesterfield Downs. Evelyn Pepper was found unconscious in the tack room this morning with a broken hip and a nasty bump on the head,' Mrs Smith began.

'Poor Miss Pepper. That's terrible. What happened to her?' Alice-Miranda asked.

'It seems she'd gone to get some gear but the light was broken. She must have tripped in the dark. Mr Wigglesworth found her. She's been taken off to hospital in Downsfordvale and will likely be there a couple of weeks. If I know Evelyn, she'll be beside herself. Chesterfield Downs won't be the same without her. She rides track work, trains all those horses and feeds everyone who works there too,' Mrs Smith explained.

'Is there anything we can do to help?' Alice-Miranda asked.

'That's what Mr Wigglesworth phoned about. He wondered if I might be able to organise some meals for them, just lunch and some afternoon tea. Which of course I can do in a heartbeat.'

'Well, I'm going to write Miss Pepper a card this afternoon. I've only met her a couple of times but Bonaparte took a real shine to her when we were riding through the village last term. And you know Bony doesn't like many people straight away. Come to think of it, Bony doesn't like many people, full stop.'

'I'm sure Evelyn would love a cheery card.' Mrs Smith stood up and glanced at the kitchen clock. 'But I think you should be on your way to class, even if it is your birthday.'

'Oh, I almost forgot. I came to ask if Millie and I could have some sandwiches to take to the stables at lunchtime, please. We want to check on Bony and

Chops and spend some time with Mr Walt before he leaves at the end of the week,' said Alice-Miranda. 'And I've got hockey practice this afternoon and a drama lesson tomorrow after school so we can't ride until at least Wednesday.'

'How does ham and a little dash of mustard, some tomato, Swiss cheese and lettuce sound?' Doreen Smith asked.

'Perfect, thank you,' Alice-Miranda replied. 'I'll see you soon.'

The child exited the kitchen through the back door and walked across the cobblestoned courtyard to her class.

Chapter 3

'I wish Wally wasn't leaving,' said Millie. She and Alice-Miranda were munching on their sandwiches as they headed for the stables.

'Yes, but he said from the time he arrived that it's been his dream to work with thoroughbreds in a racing stable,' Alice-Miranda replied.

'But why? What's wrong with ponies like Chops? Who'd want to work with a single breed when you can have twelve varieties in one special little package?'

Alice-Miranda laughed. 'Mmm . . . I can see your point.' She held her hands out as if weighing each option. 'Working with Rockstar, the most successful racehorse on the planet, or working with Chops, the laziest pony on earth.'

'Hey, don't talk about my boy like that – he's got feelings too, you know.' Millie smiled, and then thought about it a bit more. 'No, scratch that – he can't feel anything. I have to kick him so much to get him moving, I think he must have armour underneath that furry coat of his.'

Alice-Miranda giggled.

As the girls entered the cool stone building, Bonaparte let out an ear-piercing whinny and hung his head over the stall door.

'Hello to you too.' Alice-Miranda grabbed a couple of carrots from the feed room and strode over to the stall. She thrust the orange vegetables towards Bonaparte, who ignored them completely and reached out to nibble the birthday garland on Alice-Miranda's head. It was tradition to wear the flowers all day.

'Excuse me.' Alice-Miranda pulled back to see Bonaparte chewing on a purple iris, which he promptly spat onto the ground.

'That will teach you,' she chided. 'Not very tasty, I assume.'

Chops, on the other hand, was dozing, completely oblivious to the arrival of his mistress.

'Hey lazybones,' Millie called as she went to get a brush and comb from the tack room. Chops opened one eye and then closed it again.

Wally Whitstable appeared pushing an empty wheelbarrow.

'Good afternoon, girls, and happy birthday, Miss Alice-Miranda,' the lad said with a nod. He deposited the wheelbarrow into an empty stall and retrieved a rake that was leaning against the wall. 'I can't imagine those two ponies of yours being more different. Chops here has been sleeping all morning and that bloke –' he pointed an accusing finger towards Bonaparte – 'has been trying to break out of his stall. Rotten little monster almost took my hand off before *and* I was gonna give him a treat. But he can forget that now.'

'I'm so sorry,' Alice-Miranda apologised on Bonaparte's behalf. 'I thought his manners had improved lately but obviously not.'

'If you're going to work with racehorses, you'd better get used to it,' Millie piped up from inside the stall where she was combing Chops's matted mane.

'I suppose you're right there,' Wally agreed.

'When do you start your new job?' Millie asked.

'On the weekend,' Wally replied. 'But I don't want to leave Charlie in the lurch, either. He had a lad lined up to take my place here but the boy's been offered a spot at a farm in Downsfordvale that's closer to his home and so now Charlie's back to square one.'

'No doubt Mr Charles will find someone. This is such a wonderful opportunity for you, Mr Walt,' Alice-Miranda said reassuringly as she walked over to the tack room and emerged with a hoof pick. She placed her floral garland on a small table in the main part of the stables before she opened Bony's stall door, walked inside and ran her hand down his foreleg. 'Have you heard about Miss Pepper?'

'No, what about Miss Pepper?' Wally replied.

'I'm afraid she had an accident this morning and broke her hip. She's going to be in hospital for a couple of weeks,' said Alice-Miranda.

Wally winced. 'Goodness, that sounds bad. I wonder who'll be riding Rockstar now.'

'Maybe you will,' Alice-Miranda said.

'No way! I'm not riding him. Everyone says he's the meanest racehorse in the world, except with Miss Pepper. I heard he even bit Her Majesty last time she was here.'

'Oh goodness, really? Aunty Gee would have given him a big telling-off for that sort of behaviour. I think she's very proud of him, most of the time,' Alice-Miranda replied. 'She says he's the best horse she's ever had. Anyway, I think you'll have a wonderful time at Chesterfield Downs and hopefully we can come over and visit.'

'I'd like that,' Wally replied. 'Dick Wigglesworth, the stable foreman, has known me since I was a boy. He's a good fellow and I'm sure he wouldn't mind you popping in to say hello. Besides, isn't Queen Georgiana your aunty or something anyway?'

'She's Mummy's and Aunt Charlotte's godmother and Granny's best friend since kindergarten,' said Alice-Miranda.

'And she and I are like that.' Millie crossed her fingers and held them in the air. 'She gave me a hug on board the *Octavia* and you know Her Majesty doesn't just hug anyone.'

Wally laughed at the thought of Queen

Georgiana offering random hugs to strangers. He glanced at his watch.

'Hadn't you two better be getting back to class? You don't want to miss your afternoon lessons,' he said.

'I do,' Millie groaned. 'I've got PE and Miss Wall is making us run cross country. I'd rather do Jacinta's dirty laundry than run that course.'

Alice-Miranda let go of Bony's foot and ducked around under his head. She popped up hanging over the stable door. 'You know, if Charlie doesn't find someone, Millie and I can take over here for a little while. I don't mind mucking out,' she offered.

'Pooh! Speak for yourself.' Millie hauled herself up onto Chops's bare back. 'I'd rather go riding.'

'We can still ride,' Alice-Miranda said, 'but they're our ponies. We should be looking after them.'

Millie grinned mischievously. 'Maybe we can get Sloane to give us a hand.'

'I think you've got more chance of Chops winning the Queen's Cup,' Alice-Miranda giggled.

'You're right about that,' Wally nodded.

Chapter 4

On Wednesday after school Alice-Miranda and Millie saddled up their ponies and headed out for a short ride. There wasn't enough time to go on their favourite route over to Gertrude's Grove, so instead they headed in the opposite direction, down along the river to Duck's Flat.

'We should go and see Miss Hephzibah and Miss Henrietta on the weekend,' Alice-Miranda turned and called to Millie, who was having trouble getting Chops to keep up.

'Caledonia Manor looks incredible. They should be ready to open the teaching college soon,' Millie called back. She gave Chops a sharp kick in the flank, to little effect. 'I think I might retire Chops soon and start riding Stumps instead.'

Chops seemed to take this rather personally and launched himself into a fast-paced canter alongside Bonaparte, who turned his head and attempted to give the old fellow a nip.

'Bonaparte!' Alice-Miranda tugged sharply on the reins. 'Behave yourself, you naughty little beast.'

'I'm not stopping now,' Millie shouted as Chops surged forward, picking up the pace and belting off across the paddock. 'Race you to the pond.'

Alice-Miranda urged Bony into a canter and then a gallop. She liked the way the crisp afternoon air prickled her face.

Millie reached their destination first, as Alice-Miranda knew she would. Although Chops impersonated a sloth most days, when he got going there was no way Bonaparte could beat him. Millie leapt out of the saddle and led the pony to the edge of the pond for a drink. Alice-Miranda did the same and the two girls stood side by side as Bony and Chops slurped the cool water.

On the far side of the pond swam a brown mother duck followed by five fuzzy ducklings.

'Oh, they're so sweet,' said Alice-Miranda as she watched the little ones race to stay close to their mother.

Then something else caught her attention.

'Do you see that?' She tapped Millie on the shoulder and pointed.

'What?' said Millie, squinting into the distance.

'I think it's the top of a tent,' Alice-Miranda decided. 'We should go and say hello. The campers probably don't know they're on private property.'

Alice-Miranda gathered Bony's reins and led him around the edge of the pond and over the stream via an ancient stone causeway. Millie and Chops followed.

'Hello, is anyone here?' Alice-Miranda called as she approached the camp site. A two-man tent was pitched beside a scrubby bush. Wisps of smoke rose from a camp fire and beside it, a young man was sitting on a log and cooking sausages. There was a billy boiling on the fire too.

'Hello,' Alice-Miranda called again.

'Oh, hello yourself.' The fellow stood up. He was short and stocky with dark hair and tanned skin and he had the most unusual tawny-coloured eyes.

Alice-Miranda thought he looked about the same age as Mr Walt, probably late teens or early twenties.

'That smells delicious.' Alice-Miranda nodded at the sausages as they sizzled away. She held out her hand. 'My name is Alice-Miranda Highton-Smith-Kennington-Jones and I'm very pleased to meet you, Mr . . .'

She waited for an answer.

The man's brow wrinkled. 'Um.' He looked at the fire and then at her, then down at the ground. 'Billy. Billy, uh . . .' He hesitated for another moment. 'Boots, Billy Boots.' He stepped forward and took Alice-Miranda's tiny hand in his.

'Well, it's lovely to meet you, Mr Boots,' Alice-Miranda smiled. 'This is Millicent Jane McLoughlin-McTavish-McNoughton-McGill, but she prefers Millie.'

'I can see why,' said Billy. 'That's more than a mouthful.'

Millie said hello and reached forward to shake the young man's hand too.

'Are you on holiday?' Millie asked, glancing around at the camp site.

'Sort of. Bit of a boy's own adventure,' he replied. 'I'm picking up some work here and there. Finding my fortune I suppose you could say.'

'Oh,' said Alice-Miranda. 'What sort of work do you do?'

'I'm not fussy.'

And then like a lightning bolt, Alice-Miranda remembered. 'Mr Boots, are you any good with horses?'

'I've had some experience and I like 'em well enough,' he replied.

'Mr Walt is leaving us at the end of the week and we need someone to help out at the stables at school. You should come and see Mr Charles about the job. I'm not sure if he has anyone lined up but it can't hurt to ask,' Alice-Miranda fizzed. Then she stopped for a moment, frowning. 'But I don't think you can live here. I mean, it's a lovely spot to camp but I can't imagine that Miss Grimm will be very happy about it.'

'I think there's a flat above the stables,' Millie offered. 'Wally doesn't live there because he lives in the village with his parents.'

'Oh, it's too perfect for words,' said Alice-Miranda, beaming.

Billy nodded slowly. 'Yeah, it sounds all right to me, I suppose.'

Millie nudged her friend. 'Come on, we need to get going, Alice-Miranda. It's getting dark.'

'I hadn't realised it was so late,' Alice-Miranda replied. 'But why don't you come to the school tomorrow, Mr Boots, and ask to speak with Mr Charles Weatherly. I'll let him know that Millie and I met you. Probably best to head over about morning tea time – that's eleven o'clock.'

Billy reached out to give Bonaparte a pat. Bony bared his teeth, and then did the strangest thing. He licked Billy's arm.

'Oi, what are you doing!' The young man pulled away.

'Bony!' Alice-Miranda giggled and tugged firmly on his reins. 'That's very strange. I'm sorry but that means he likes you. And believe me, he really doesn't like most people at all – especially young men.'

'I'll take your word for it,' said Billy, frowning at the pony. 'They're not all like him are they?'

'Oh no, not at all,' Alice-Miranda replied. 'The other ponies are much friendlier.'

The two girls hauled themselves into the saddles and wheeled Bony and Chops around.

'See you tomorrow,' Alice-Miranda called.

'Yeah, tomorrow.' Billy raised his chin in a sort of backwards nod.

Millie and Alice-Miranda made it back to the stables with just enough time to give Bony and Chops a quick rub down and some food before the girls were due at their evening meal. As they were finishing up, Wally Whitstable and Charlie Weatherly drove up in the four-wheel drive with a fresh load of straw on board.

Alice-Miranda met them as they got out of the vehicle. 'Hello Mr Charles, Mr Walt. I'm glad that we've run into you.'

'Did you have a good ride?' Charlie asked.

'Yes, thank you,' Alice-Miranda nodded.

Millie appeared from the tack room where she had just put Chops's saddle away.

'Good afternoon, Miss Millie,' Charlie said with a nod at the red-haired girl.

'Hello Charlie. Did Alice-Miranda tell you that we met a young man camping down near Duck's Flat?' Millie asked. 'He's on an adventure.'

Charlie's brow puckered. 'What sort of an adventure?'

'I'm not really sure,' Alice-Miranda answered. 'But he was friendly and he said that he was looking for work.'

'Is the fella any good with horses?' Wally piped up.

'He said that he's had some experience and he likes them and so I thought perhaps he might be able to help out here – even if just for a little while,' Alice-Miranda suggested.

Charlie smiled at this tiny child with her cascading chocolate curls and brown eyes as big as saucers. He wondered if there was any problem she couldn't solve.

'I suggested to Mr Boots that he should come over around morning tea time tomorrow,' Alice-Miranda said.

'Sounds good, don't you think, Charlie?' said Wally eagerly.

'We'll see,' the older man replied. 'You two girls had best be getting off to dinner and if Wally ever wants to go home tonight we'd better unload this straw.'

Chapter 5

After a chat with Charles Weatherly, Billy Boots was offered a job and moved into the flat above the stables on Thursday afternoon. It was up to Wally to show the lad the ropes and make sure he was aware of all the tasks that needed doing. Wally decided he was friendly enough but very quiet, the sort of fellow who didn't want to talk much about himself. When Wally asked him about this adventure he was on, Billy changed the subject. When Wally asked where he came from, he just said, 'Up north.' There was something about him that niggled, but Wally really couldn't say what it was. He felt like he'd seen him somewhere before, but Billy insisted that this was his first time in the village.

In truth, Wally was just relieved that there was someone to take his place. It didn't matter if he was talkative or not. Looking after the stables at Winchesterfield-Downsfordvale was a much bigger job than Wally had first imagined and he hated the thought of Charlie having to take it all on again. The poor man had enough to do tending the gardens and cultivating all those prize orchids.

On Friday after school, Alice-Miranda had found Wally in the tack room oiling saddles and lured him to the dining room, with the excuse that Mr Charles needed him for some urgent last-minute chores. But of course it was all a set-up and the girls had organised a special afternoon tea to wish him well at his new job. Wally left Winchesterfield-Downsfordvale with a huge smile and promises of a visit over the weekend from Alice-Miranda and Millie.

On Saturday morning the residents of Grimthorpe House were busy getting ready for the various activities they had planned for the day. The cavernous downstairs bathroom sweated under the steam of constant showers while girls jostled for mirror space.

'What are you doing today?' Alice-Miranda asked Jacinta, who was busily brushing her teeth.

'Ma muvva tak me ut,' she said, before spitting a mouthful of frothy toothpaste and water into the sink.

'Did you say that your mother is taking you out?' Alice-Miranda repeated.

'Yes.' Jacinta wiped her face with her towel and grimaced.

'But that's lovely,' Alice-Miranda enthused.

'We'll see. Sloane's coming with me, just in case Mummy is foul.'

Alice-Miranda shook her head. 'I bet you'll have lots of fun. Your mother was pretty upset about you being abducted on board the *Octavia*. I'm sure she's changed for the better.'

The tall girl shrugged. Jacinta knew that a couple of visits didn't mean Ambrosia was in the running for mother of the year. But underneath her bravado, she was rather hoping that their relationship had turned a corner.

Jacinta stared into the foggy mirror as Sloane

appeared in the bathroom. 'Hey, what are you wearing?' she growled.

'Uh, a *dress*,' Sloane replied.

'But that's *my* dress,' Jacinta snapped.

'You said that I could wear anything in your wardrobe, so I chose this.' Sloane stared back at Jacinta in the mirror.

'It looks lovely,' said Alice-Miranda.

'I don't remember saying that,' Jacinta pouted.

'I do,' Millie piped up from the other side of a shower cubicle where she had just turned off the tap. 'You said it at lunch the other day.'

Jacinta was cornered.

'If you don't want me to wear it, I can find something else,' Sloane offered.

Jacinta looked as if she'd been struck by lightning. 'Really? You'll change?'

'Of course. I only wore it because when you unwrapped the parcel from your mother last week you didn't seem to like it very much. You've got heaps of clothes in that enormous wardrobe of yours,' Sloane said. 'I'll find something else.'

'Well, I would like to wear it,' said Jacinta, watching Sloane carefully.

Millie emerged with a towel wrapped around

her and a cute shower cap covered in ponies on her head. She and Alice-Miranda exchanged smiles. Jacinta and Sloane had certainly both come a long way lately.

Sloane glanced at Alice-Miranda, who was wearing jodhpurs and a shirt. 'I suppose you're spending the day on that nag of yours?' The blonde girl tousled her hair with her fingers and then pulled a brush out of her toiletries bag.

'Yes,' Alice-Miranda nodded. 'First we're going to see Miss Hephzibah and Miss Henrietta and have a look at what's been happening at Caledonia Manor, and then we're going to ride over and visit Mr Walt at Chesterfield Downs. If there's time we'll go to Fayle and say hello to Lucas and Sep but that might have to wait until tomorrow. We should do some proper training for the show too. We're going to enter all the pairs events in hacking and then I think we should try the barrel racing and keyhole too – they're loads of fun.'

Sloane wrinkled her nose. 'I can't imagine. And don't bother going to Fayle. Lucas and Sep are out on some horrible cadet camp this weekend. Do you think there could be anything more revolting than traipsing around the woods pretending to be soldiers?'

'It sounds like fun to me,' said Alice-Miranda. 'What are you two doing?'

'Ambrosia's taking us to the movies and then to have milkshakes,' said Sloane, looking pleased with herself. 'But say hello to Granny Henrietta and tell her I'll get over and visit her soon.'

Alice-Miranda nodded. 'We will.'

One by one the girls finished their morning ablutions and headed back to their rooms.

Alice-Miranda and Millie said goodbye to Jacinta and Sloane and raced off to the stables. There was no sign of anyone about so the girls tacked up the ponies and wrote a note on the blackboard indicating their plans.

'I wonder where Mr Boots is,' said Alice-Miranda as she nimbly threw her leg over Bonaparte.

'He must be some kind of superman,' Millie commented, looking around at the stalls with their fresh straw. The tack room was positively gleaming and there wasn't a thing out of place. 'I hate to say it but he makes Wally look lazier than Chops.'

Alice-Miranda clicked her tongue and Bonaparte

walked out into the bright sunshine. Millie was having a quiet word in Chops's ear. Whatever she said must have worked because as soon as they were outside he began to trot.

The two girls decided they would take their favourite route over to Gertrude's Grove, have their morning tea there and then head to Caledonia Manor. Mrs Smith had supplied them with a lovely spread comprised of roast beef sandwiches, poppy seed cake, apples and a couple of chocolate-iced cupcakes thrown in for good measure. Millie was carrying it all in a small leather satchel attached to the side of Chops's saddle.

The ponies walked and trotted through the woods before they reached the clearing that led up over a rise and then down to Gertrude's Grove. Millie challenged Alice-Miranda to a race and the two girls found themselves cantering along, enjoying the warm sun on their faces and the breeze in their hair. But just as Millie reached the top of the hill, she tugged violently at Chops's reins and the pony came to a jerky halt. Alice-Miranda pulled up beside her.

'What's the matter? Why did you stop?' she asked.

'Look down there.' Millie pointed at an array of vehicles: trucks and trailers, caravans and the odd car. The whole of the flat beside the stream had been transformed into a giant camping ground.

'I wonder who they are,' said Alice-Miranda.

'Carnies,' Millie replied.

'You mean show people? The ones who run all the rides and things at the show?' Alice-Miranda asked.

'Yup.' Millie began to wheel Chops around.

'Where are you going?' Alice-Miranda asked.

Millie wrinkled her nose. 'We can't go down there now.'

'Why ever not?' Alice-Miranda asked.

'Because they're *carnies*,' Millie said.

'But what's wrong with them?' Alice-Miranda turned Bonaparte back around and scanned the impromptu camp site.

'I don't know exactly, but I heard Charlie telling Howie last year that they weren't to be trusted,' Millie said. 'I think there were some robberies around the village when the show was on. But I don't think Constable Derby ever caught anyone.'

Alice-Miranda had never met anyone who ran a carnival before. 'That's a bit unfair, don't you think

– blaming the carnival people? It could have been anyone. And if they're so terrible, how come everyone loves it when the carnival comes to town? These people earn their living making children happy. If they were really dangerous, surely they wouldn't be welcome at all.'

Millie thought about it for a moment. Her friend had a point. 'Maybe we should just go and see Miss Hephzibah and Miss Henrietta?' she suggested. 'And we can meet the carnival people another time.'

'Look,' said Alice-Miranda, pointing. 'There are some children. I think they're playing a game. Come on, don't you want to say hello?'

Millie shrugged. Before she had time to protest, Alice-Miranda and Bonaparte were trotting towards the group of youngsters who were running around in a large clearing beside the caravans.

'Alice-Miranda,' Millie called, but her words were carried away on the breeze. There was only one thing for it. Millie kicked Chops in the flank and raced to catch up.

Chapter 6

As Bonaparte jogged towards the caravans, Alice-Miranda could see a group of about ten children kicking a ball. A chubby girl standing on the sideline looked up and pointed at her, then shouted something, and the game came to an abrupt halt. All eyes were on the two ponies and their riders.

'Hello,' Alice-Miranda called and waved.

'Hello,' the small girl who had first spotted them called back. 'Who are you?'

Alice-Miranda slid down from the saddle and

walked Bonaparte over to where the group was standing. She undid the strap on her helmet and took it off.

'My name's Alice-Miranda Highton-Smith-Kennington-Jones. And that's my friend, Millicent Jane McLoughlin-McTavish-McNoughton-McGill, but she prefers Millie.'

'Hi,' Millie called and waved. She dismounted too and pulled the reins over Chops's head.

'Geez, listen to you two with your posh names and your posh-lookin' ponies. I suppose you're probably related to the Queen too,' a tall boy sneered.

'No, Aunty Gee's not a blood relative but she is Mummy's godmother,' Alice-Miranda replied.

The boy rolled his eyes.

'What's your name?' Alice-Miranda asked him.

'If you must know, Miss Nosey, I'm Pete and he's Robbie and he's Jim and that's Lola and Fern and Rory and Stephen and Indigo and Nick and Ellie.' He pointed at them all one by one. 'And that little pest there –' he waved a finger at the chubby girl – 'is Ivy.'

She poked her tongue out at him. 'Am not a pest!' Ivy was holding a tatty doll. It had matted hair and was missing an arm.

'I'm sorry, but I don't know if I'll be able to remember all your names straight away.' Alice-Miranda looked at Ivy and her doll. 'You must love her a lot.'

The small child nodded.

'What are the ponies called?' Ivy asked.

'He's Bonaparte,' Alice-Miranda replied, 'and that's Chops.'

'What a daft name for a horse,' Pete scoffed. 'In't that a brand of dog food?'

'So what if it is?' Millie retorted.

'I'm getting a pony,' Ivy said.

'No, you're not,' Pete snapped. 'Where are we gonna put a pony? All the rides round here are mechanical. You know how much Alf hates havin' more mouths to feed.'

At the mention of the name 'Alf', a suffocating silence fell over the group. Alice-Miranda wondered if he was in charge of the carnival, and why his name had such an effect.

'Can we play?' Alice-Miranda asked as she glanced around and spied the scuffed football that the boy called Rory was holding.

'What do you think?' Pete asked the other kids. 'Should we let the poshos play? Reckon they're any good?'

'Oh, I'm afraid I'm not,' Alice-Miranda said, 'but Millie's fantastic.'

'All right, let's pick the teams again. Rory, you can be the captain for the Rangers and I'm the captain for the Stars. I'm going first. I want Robbie.' Pete pointed at the boy with dark curls.

'Stephen.' Rory pointed at a kid with closely cropped blond hair.

'I want li'l Jimmy,' Pete continued.

Rory pointed. 'Nick.'

'Hey, what about the girls?' Indigo called out. 'It's not fair. You always pick the boys first.'

'Indigo, you're with us.' Pete pointed at her and she smiled.

'Lola,' said Rory.

'Fern,' said Pete.

'Ellie,' said Rory.

'Red.' Pete pointed at Millie.

Millie rolled her eyes. 'My name's Millie.'

'Yeah, whatever,' Pete replied. 'I'm calling you Red.'

'Alice-whatever-your-name-is,' said Rory.

'What about me?' Ivy whined.

Rory shook his head. 'No, the teams are even. You can't play.'

'That's not fair!' Ivy stamped her foot and threw her doll on the ground. 'I'm going to tell my dad on you, Rory.'

Rory relented. 'All right, you can be the ref, then.'

Ivy turned around and smiled with all her teeth. 'You gotta give me the whistle.'

Rory sighed. 'Just don't lose it or you're buying me a new one.' He took a whistle on a string from around his neck and placed it around Ivy's.

'Are they playing too?' Pete asked, looking at the ponies. Millie and Alice-Miranda were holding their reins loosely and the hungry pair were now chomping on the long clumps of grass which grew on the edge of the field.

Alice-Miranda laughed. 'Oh, I don't think so. Bony would be much too competitive. Come on, mister.' She pulled hard on the reins and managed to get Bonaparte's head out of the grass. Millie did the same and the girls walked the ponies over to the fence and hitched their reins to the wire. On the other side, along the bank of the stream, a stand of willow trees swayed lazily in the breeze like a row of hula dancers.

'I suppose they seem okay,' Millie whispered to Alice-Miranda.

'Bony and Chops will be fine here,' Alice-Miranda nodded.

'I meant those kids. Except that one who keeps calling me Red.'

'Oh.' Alice-Miranda smiled at Millie. 'Maybe he just couldn't remember your name.'

The teams lined up against one another. Sticks at either end of the field marked out goalposts. Other than that there were no lines. It was up to Ivy to blow the whistle when she thought there was an infringement. Rory had won the toss and as Ivy blew the whistle, the lad kicked off. He shot the ball backwards to Stephen, who dribbled it down the pitch before running into Pete, who stole the ball and kicked it to Robbie, who was quickly cornered by Rory and Nick.

'Over here,' the thin girl with dark hair called.

'Fern!' Robbie shouted and booted it towards her. She dribbled the ball up the field, managing to dodge Rory, then Stephen. She was close to the goal.

'Don't let her score,' Nick yelled. 'Get the ball!'

Before anyone had time to tackle her, Fern struck the ball and it flew through the two sticks.

A cheer went up from Pete's Stars, who leapt about, slapping each other on the back. Pete pulled his shirt over his head like the footballers on television and ran around with his arms outstretched like an aeroplane's wings. Fern gave Millie a huge smile before high-fiving her.

The game continued for about ten minutes with Rory's Rangers scoring the next two goals. Alice-Miranda had only kicked the ball once but she was enjoying running around the field.

Rory booted the ball hard and it flew past the ponies and through the fence.

'I'll get it,' said Alice-Miranda.

She ran to the fence and ducked through the wires that divided Gertrude's Grove from the stream. She scanned the bank for the ball but couldn't see it. A couple of thick shrubs grew close to the water's edge. Alice-Miranda scampered along the bank and was just about to check under the shrubs when she noticed a boy sitting a little further downstream on a flat rock. She thought he looked about the same age as Lucas and Sep, and he was engrossed in something.

'Hello,' Alice-Miranda called. The boy glanced up at her but quickly focused back on whatever it was he'd been looking at.

'Oh, goodness!' Alice-Miranda exclaimed. 'What a lovely lot of badges you've got there.'

Sitting on the rock in neat rows were at least forty badges of all different shapes, colours and sizes. Beside them was a plastic drawstring bag.

The boy pointed to the badges one at a time as he said, 'That's from the fire brigade. It's an Inspector's badge from 1978 and that's the Queen's Guards badge from 1985 and that one Fern got from Chicken Charlie's last year.'

Alice-Miranda read the name on another badge and wondered who Sylvia Rutherford was.

The boy looked up at her and she noticed that he had the most extraordinary amber-coloured eyes, like one of Miss Hephzibah's cats.

'My name is Alice-Miranda Highton-Smith-Kennington-Jones.' She offered her hand, which he completely ignored. 'What's your name?'

His attention went back to the badges.

'Tarquin James Sharlan,' he said.

'Well, it's lovely to meet you Tarquin James Sharlan. I'm looking for the football,' Alice-Miranda explained. She was surprised the other children hadn't come after her by now. She spied the ball under a bush close to the boy, reached in and pulled it out. 'Do you want to play?'

'Not allowed,' the boy said, staring at his collection. 'They won't let me.'

'Why don't you come back with me and we'll see what they say?'

Tarquin began to put his treasures away in the drawstring bag. He counted the badges as he placed them carefully inside.

'Do you want some help with that?' Alice-Miranda reached down to assist.

'Don't touch!' he snapped. 'I can do it.'

Alice-Miranda backed away and watched him finish packing his belongings. He dusted each badge before placing it carefully into the bag. Alice-Miranda finally emerged from the bushes with Tarquin behind her.

'About time,' Rory yelled. 'We were gonna send a search party.'

Pete spied Tarquin. 'Oh, what's he doing here?' he sighed.

'I thought he could join the game,' said Alice-Miranda as she ran onto the field. Tarquin hung back near the fence.

'No way,' Rory said.

'Why not?' Alice-Miranda asked.

'Because he's weird,' Pete said.

The children had now gathered around Alice-Miranda.

'He is not!' Fern spat.

'Is too,' Robbie said.

'He can play if he wants,' Fern said firmly.

'Sides won't be even then,' Pete said.

From the other side of the temporary fairground came a wailing cry, like a banshee with a bee-sting. 'Jimmy Peterson, you get off that field and come and clean up your rubbish.'

Jimmy sighed. 'I gotta go, or she'll be out here dragging me by the ear.' He scampered off towards the camp.

Alice-Miranda looked at Pete. 'Now you need another player for your team.'

'Tarq, come on,' Fern called to the boy.

Alice-Miranda noticed that Fern's eyes were almost the exact same colour as Tarquin's. She had a similar olive complexion and dark hair too.

Tarquin ran towards the field.

'What about me?' Ivy whined. 'I don't want to be the referee any more. It's boring.'

'I'll swap if you like,' Ellie offered.

Ivy gave her the whistle and skipped back to find a position.

'He has to be the goalie,' said Pete, making a face at Tarquin. 'And you'd better not let any through.'

Tarquin meandered off to the other end of the field and stood between the makeshift posts. Pete kicked off and with Robbie making a clear run, it looked like his team was set for another goal to draw the match. Just as Robbie struck the ball towards the posts, Nick intercepted and ran the full length of the field.

Pete looked at the empty goal. 'Where's Tarquin?' he yelled angrily.

Tarquin had disappeared and was now sitting on the sideline examining a stick.

Nick flew towards the goals and kicked. Score!

Rory's Rangers were leading three to one.

'I told you he's an idiot,' said Pete, storming towards Tarquin.

'Leave him alone,' Fern yelled. 'He didn't mean it.'

Pete grabbed Tarquin by the shirt and shook him.

'Stop it!' Fern screamed. The rest of the kids ran to see what was going on.

Alice-Miranda tried to reason with him. 'Please, Pete. I'm sure that Tarquin was just distracted.'

'What would you know?' Pete yelled at her. 'You don't know him. You don't know anything about him. Someone needs to teach him a lesson.' Pete picked up the bag containing Tarquin's badge collection.

'NO!' the boy yelled and snatched it back again.

'Why, you!' Pete reached out to push Tarquin but Fern got in the way. He shoved her with all his might and she fell to the ground, taking the full weight on her left wrist.

Tarquin rushed at Pete. Alice-Miranda tried to stop him but Pete flung her out of the way like a rag doll. The tiny girl fell, grazing her forehead on a sharp stone that was hidden in the grass.

'Pete, stop it!' Rory yelled. 'Alf's coming. If he catches you fighting you know what he'll do.'

'Go and play with your stupid badges,' Pete yelled at Tarquin, who immediately sprang to his feet and ran towards the fence, nimbly negotiating the wires and disappearing through the willows.

Pete reached out to help Alice-Miranda up.

She felt the sting of tears in her eyes and her head hurt a little but she grabbed his hand.

'You shouldn't have done that,' he said. 'You shouldn't have interfered.' Then without another word, the group scattered and Pete ran off towards the caravans and out of sight.

Fern lay on the ground. She was holding her wrist and crying quietly.

'That Pete's a brute,' said Millie. She reached out to help Fern stand. 'You should see the doctor about your wrist. It might be broken.'

The raven-haired girl cradled her injured hand against her chest. 'It's nothing,' she insisted, sniffing.

'We could at least get you some ice,' Alice-Miranda suggested.

'No! You've done enough. Just go away. You don't belong here!' With that the girl fled towards the camp site and disappeared into the maze of vehicles.

Alice-Miranda and Millie were left alone in the middle of the field.

'Are you all right? You're bleeding,' said Millie. She pulled a tissue from her pocket and reached up to put it against Alice-Miranda's forehead. 'I can't believe he pushed you.'

'It's just a scratch,' said Alice-Miranda, 'and I think he was sorry.'

'Come on.' Millie put her arm around Alice-Miranda and the girls walked towards the ponies. 'We should go and see Miss Hephzibah. I'm sure she'll have a plaster.'

The bloody mark on Alice-Miranda's forehead was beginning to swell.

'I told you the carnies can't be trusted,' Millie grumbled as she gave Alice-Miranda a leg-up onto Bonaparte's back.

'It was just a stupid argument,' Alice-Miranda said, frowning. But she had a strange feeling about Tarquin and the children from the carnival.

Millie threw her leg over Chops. 'Let's go.'

The girls wheeled their ponies around and began to trot up the hill away from the camp site. Alice-Miranda turned to look back and saw Fern sitting on the step of a whitewashed caravan. It was the biggest of all in the camp. In front of her a giant of a man with a ginger beard was making extravagant gestures. He didn't look happy. She wondered if he was the fellow they called Alf.

Millie and Alice-Miranda rode back through the woods and turned right at the fork in the road, towards Caledonia Manor. They didn't stop at the stables but rode up the driveway. The place was completely transformed since Alice-Miranda's last visit over a month ago. Back then the builders and tradesmen had been busy concentrating on the renovations to the manor. The gardens had still been overgrown with waist-high weeds, but now the grounds were splendid.

'Look at that.' Millie pointed at a gigantic fountain in the middle of the lawn. Water spurted from the ornate cherub centrepiece.

'It must have been there all the time,' Alice-Miranda said. 'You just couldn't see it. And don't those flowerbeds look lovely?' Alice-Miranda studied the pretty blooms growing along the fence.

The front of the manor, with its four Ionic columns and stately portico, looked as grand as ever. The double doors were painted slate grey and the brass handles gleamed.

'We should go around the back and tie the ponies up there,' Millie suggested. 'That's where I've left Chops when I've been to visit.'

They passed by the side of the mansion with its new roof and rebuilt wing. Alice-Miranda couldn't help thinking that the house looked twice as large as it had before the renovations.

The girls rode across the expansive lawn to the bottom row of balustrades and slid off their ponies, hitching them to the railing.

A crust of dried blood had formed on Alice-Miranda's forehead and the bump was notice-ably larger than when they had left Gertrude's Grove.

Millie pointed at the wound. 'You really need someone to take a look at that.'

'I'm fine. Really I am. It doesn't hurt at – ow!' Alice-Miranda flinched as she reached up and touched her head. 'All right. It hurts a little bit,' she confessed.

The girls made their way to the kitchen door. Several cats were asleep in sunny spots along the veranda. A grey tabby woke at their approach and stretched out.

'Hello puss,' said Alice-Miranda. She reached down and gave its belly a rub.

'Miss Hephzibah, Miss Henrietta,' Millie called as she knocked loudly, then opened the screen door.

The girls could see the outline of Hephzibah standing beside the stove.

'Oh Millie, what a lovely surprise, and Alice-Miranda too. Heavens, dear, whatever happened to you?' Hephzibah called as she caught sight of Alice-Miranda. She ushered both children inside and ordered Alice-Miranda to take a seat at the kitchen table.

Chapter 7

Hephzibah bustled about the kitchen, insistent that for once Alice-Miranda should sit quite still. The old woman found a first aid kit in the butler's pantry and swabbed Alice-Miranda's grazed forehead with antiseptic. A bandaid covered the wound. Then she wrapped some ice in a tea towel and told Alice-Miranda to hold it on her forehead for a little while to help the swelling.

'Now, I'll make us some tea,' said Hephzibah. 'Do stay *still*, dear!'

'Is Miss Henrietta home?' Alice-Miranda asked.

'Not at the moment. Mrs Parker came this morning to take her for her doctor's appointment. Ever since you "discovered" me here and I came out for all the world to see, Mrs Parker's been so kind and helpful,' Hephzibah said as she busied herself locating three teacups and saucers in the cupboard.

'Mrs Parker?' Millie asked distastefully. 'Do you mean Myrtle Parker?'

'Yes, Millie,' Hephzibah nodded. 'Why do you ask?'

'You must be one of the only people in the village who has anything nice to say about her,' Millie said. 'She's a bit of a busybody.'

'Oh no, Millie. She's lovely – always terribly interested in what's happening. I don't know how I would have managed without her help,' the old woman said. 'And Henny has come to rely on her quite a bit too.'

Millie still looked unconvinced. 'She didn't get the nickname Nosey for nothing.'

'I haven't met her yet,' Alice-Miranda said.

'You will soon enough,' said Millie. 'She's the president of the Show Society and Mrs Howard says that she's the village's self-appointed expert on everything. She's even given herself the job of chief judge for all of the equestrian events, which isn't going to be good for Chops, seeing that when I was out riding in the village earlier in the year she told me he looked like a cross between a donkey and a Dartmoor pony. As if! He's got at least another ten varieties in him. Silly woman wouldn't know her ponies from her pigs, I say.'

Hephzibah and Alice-Miranda giggled.

'Is Miss Henrietta well?' Alice-Miranda asked, changing the subject.

'She's made some remarkable progress since that terrible stroke. The doctors can hardly believe it,' the old woman replied.

Hephzibah poured three cups of tea, black for herself and weak and milky for the two girls. She placed them on the table and pushed the sugar bowl towards Alice-Miranda.

'Thank you, Miss Hephzibah.' Alice-Miranda put a teaspoon of sugar into her cup.

Millie reached over and dumped three large scoops into her tea.

'Are you making syrup?' Alice-Miranda asked.

'Ha ha,' Millie replied. 'I'm not going to stir it.'

Hephzibah smiled. 'You know, I used to like it just like that myself when I was a girl.'

'See, Alice-Miranda, there are other people who have good taste, you know,' Millie said with a nod.

Hephzibah looked across at Alice-Miranda, her cornflower blue eyes sparkling. 'So, tell me, how *did* you come to get that bump on your head? I hope that naughty pony of yours didn't have anything to do with it.'

'It was nothing, really,' Alice-Miranda replied.

'If you don't tell, then I will,' Millie threatened.

'Okay . . .' Alice-Miranda explained all about their meeting with the children from the carnival and the lovely time they were having playing football. She told Hephzibah about finding Tarquin by the stream and his collection of badges. Millie took great delight in joining in the tale.

'. . . Pete went off his head and said that Tarquin was stupid, and Fern said that he wasn't, and then she got in the way and Pete pushed her over and she hurt her wrist, and then when Alice-Miranda tried to help, Pete pushed her so hard! And she hit her forehead on a rock in the grass. I warned Alice-Miranda that the carnies weren't to be trusted but she just wouldn't listen . . .'

Alice-Miranda protested that it wasn't anything

near as bad as Millie said. Miss Hephzibah nodded and sipped her tea quietly.

After a minute or so, the old woman broke the silence. 'I think I know better than most what it feels like to be an outsider. Those carnival children do too.' She put a hand to her scarred cheek and her eyes took on a glassy sheen.

Alice-Miranda walked around the table to Miss Hephzibah, gave the woman a hug and pecked her powdered cheek.

'Now what was that for?' Hephzibah asked.

'Just because,' Alice-Miranda smiled.

Hephzibah hugged Alice-Miranda back.

'Well, I still don't think we should go anywhere near the Grove for the next couple of weeks,' Millie said decisively. 'And I hope we don't see those kids again.'

But Alice-Miranda couldn't stop thinking about Fern and Tarquin. She wondered if they were brother and sister. They certainly looked alike. She was hoping very much to see them again, and sooner rather than later.

The girls helped clear their cups and saucers, and Hephzibah offered to take them on a tour of the house.

'When does the teaching college open?' Millie asked as the threesome walked from the kitchen into the grand foyer.

'It's still a little way off – but I know Miss Grimm and Professor Winterbottom have been interviewing for staff,' the old woman replied. 'There's a bit of government red tape they have to pass yet.'

Through crystal clear windows, shards of light danced on the polished parquet floor. Long gone were the white dust sheets that had covered the furniture and hidden Caledonia Manor's splendour. The grand entrance foyer was truly magnificent. Its stairway rose up in the centre of the room and then splayed into two flights going left and right. A silk carpet runner in red and blue ran up both sides. An array of ornate antiques adorned the room, including a grandfather clock with the most delightful chime. There was a mahogany table against the left-hand wall, and in the middle of it an enormous floral display in an antique Japanese urn gave a splash of colour to the vast room. From the centre of the ceiling a crystal chandelier twinkled.

'It's beautiful,' Alice-Miranda gasped.

'Yes,' said Hephzibah. 'It's the showpiece of the whole house.'

The trio continued their excursion, looking at all the improvements and renovations that had been made before returning down the back stairs to the kitchen. The screen door opened just as they arrived.

'Heph, dear, we're home,' Henrietta called as she shuffled through the door with a thickset woman following close at heel. 'Oh, hello there girls,' Henrietta smiled at Alice-Miranda and Millie. 'How lovely to see you both. Did you enjoy your visit to New York, Alice-Miranda? You know Mrs Parker, I presume.'

Myrtle Parker wore an extraordinary old-fashioned pillbox hat with a veil across the top of her face and a matching floral dress which enhanced her already generous proportions, making her look a little like an overstuffed couch.

'Hello Mrs Parker, I don't believe we *have* met before. My name is Alice-Miranda Highton-Smith-Kennington-Jones.' Alice-Miranda held out her hand, which Myrtle took into her gloved grip.

'I know *exactly* who you are, my dear. And I can't imagine for a second how you have managed to avoid me these past months since you arrived, early might I add, at Winchesterfield-Downsfordvale. You've had quite the adventurous year too, with that lovely cruise on board the *Octavia* and then your recent sojourn to New York. Did you enjoy Mrs Kimmel's?' Mrs Parker asked with a wide smile.

'Goodness, Mrs Parker, you certainly are well informed,' said Alice-Miranda. She glanced quickly at Hephzibah, who was frowning, and Millie who had her best 'I told you so' face on.

Myrtle Parker turned her attention to the flame-haired girl. 'Millicent, it's nice to see you. I hear that your grandfather Ambrose has been keeping very close company with Alice-Miranda's family cook. Mrs Oliver is indeed a lucky woman to have garnered the affection of that charming man. I didn't think he'd ever get over the loss of your grandmother. She was a darling woman, although she had a tendency to be a little too concerned with other people's business.'

Millie's eyes almost popped out of her head. 'Excuse me?'

'I don't mean to speak ill of the departed, Millicent, but she didn't even live here in the village and she seemed to know everything about everyone,' Mrs Parker explained.

Alice-Miranda could sense Millie's discomfort. 'Well, it's been lovely to meet you, Mrs Parker, and you're looking very well, Miss Henrietta. Sloane said that she would pop over soon to see you. I think we need to get going. We have another visit to make.'

Millie stared at Myrtle Parker, her eyes narrowed.

'Where are you heading off to, girls?' Henrietta asked.

'We're going to say hello to Mr Walt at Chesterfield Downs,' Alice-Miranda explained. 'It's his first day and he was a little nervous. And I want to meet Rockstar. I hear he's the most impressive thoroughbred.'

'Well, that's a business, isn't it?' Myrtle Parker snorted. 'I'm going to see dear Evelyn Pepper over at the hospital in Downsfordvale this afternoon, but I have to confess that I'm not looking forward to it. That's where my Reginald was for all those months, God rest his weary soul.'

Hephzibah and Henrietta exchanged puzzled glances. It was the first they'd heard that Mr Parker had passed away. They would have to ask Myrtle more after the girls had gone.

'Apparently Evelyn fell because the lights were out in the tack room. Mr Wigglesworth was supposed to get the electrician in a week ago,' said Mrs Parker, raising her eyebrows so high they almost touched her hat. 'But you didn't hear that from me, ladies.'

Hephzibah suggested that Henrietta and Mrs Parker sit down and she would make them both some tea and a sandwich.

'We should be going,' Alice-Miranda said once more. The tiny child gave Henrietta and Hephzibah farewell hugs. Millie followed suit.

Myrtle Parker stared at the girls, frowning. 'So where's mine?'

Alice-Miranda leaned in to embrace the floral-clad woman who smelt of powder and tart perfume.

Myrtle Parker gripped the child tightly to her chest.

When she finally let go, Myrtle pointed at her rouged cheek, which Alice-Miranda dutifully kissed.

Millie watched the scene and knew what was required of her but her feet seemed set in concrete.

'Millicent, have you got a kiss for Aunty Myrtle?'

Millie gulped. Alice-Miranda gave her a gentle push and she too was taken into the woman's formidable grip. Millie pecked at Mrs Parker's cheek like a chicken in a farmyard, then wiped her mouth.

'And what happened to your face, Alice-Miranda?' Myrtle asked.

'It's nothing, Mrs Parker,' the child replied.

'It doesn't look like nothing. There must be a story behind it,' the woman insisted. 'You might like to tell me, Millicent.' She stared at Millie, who kept her mouth clamped shut.

Hephzibah moved her head ever so slightly from side to side, then said, 'Well, girls, off you go now, or poor Wally will think you've abandoned him.'

Hephzibah ushered them out of the kitchen and onto the back veranda. 'I think I'm beginning to understand what you mean about Mrs Parker, Millie,' the old woman whispered to the girls as she glanced back inside.

'I don't think it would do any good at all to have Mrs Parker worrying about the carnival people,' said Alice-Miranda.

Hephzibah nodded. 'On that, my dear, I completely agree.'

Chapter 8

'I'm starving,' Millie complained as the girls trotted down the drive. She looked around for the satchel containing their picnic feast.

'It's gone,' Millie groaned.

'What's gone?' Alice-Miranda asked.

'The satchel,' Millie replied. 'I thought I'd done it up properly but that dodgy buckle must have broken.'

'We could ask Miss Hephzibah for something to eat,' Alice-Miranda suggested, as they hadn't yet reached the bottom of the drive.

Millie shook her head. 'No, let's go back to school. I couldn't stand listening to any more of Nosey Parker.'

'She certainly does know a lot about people,' Alice-Miranda agreed, 'but I'm sure she has good intentions.'

'Good intentions! Pah.' Millie tightened the reins on Chops and dug her heels into his belly. He started to canter and she almost slipped off. 'Hey, what did you do that for?'

'You asked him to,' Alice-Miranda called out.

'Yes, but you know Chops isn't the most obedient pony,' Millie replied. 'It usually takes at least three or four kicks to get him to move.'

'Well, I think he's been an angel today. Did you put some molasses in his dinner last night?'

'No, but I did whisper in his ear that if he didn't start to behave better we might take a visit to the dog food factory,' Millie replied.

'Oh, Millie, that's horrible. Poor Chops.' Alice-Miranda turned her attention to the shaggy pony. 'You know she'd never do it and if she tried, I'd take you home to the Hall and you could play with Shergar and Phinnie and darling Boo.' She was referring to the other horses who spent their days grazing on the emerald fields at her home, Highton Hall.

Chops whinnied as if to agree with her and threw his head back and forth.

The girls arrived at the stables and decided to turn Bony and Chops out into the paddock for half an hour while they visited Mrs Smith.

On seeing Alice-Miranda with a bandaid on her forehead, Doreen Smith was positively overcome.

'Oh, my dear girl, what happened to you?' she fussed.

For the second time that day Alice-Miranda explained about their adventure at Gertrude's Grove and for the second time Millie took great joy in adding extra details and then admitted that somewhere she'd lost their lovely picnic lunch too.

'You sit down right there.' Mrs Smith pointed at the stool beside the bench. 'I'll make you both some roast beef sandwiches and then, when they've cooled down –' she opened the oven and pulled out a tray of her signature chocolate brownies – 'you can have one of these.'

Millie's stomach grumbled on cue. 'Yum, they smell delicious.'

'I'll have to tell Charlie about those carnival

folk,' Mrs Smith said as she opened the fridge and pulled out some butter and a slab of roast beef. 'It's a nervous time of year.'

'Why do you say that, Mrs Smith?' Alice-Miranda asked.

'Last year there was a spate of thefts around the village. They were only silly things like garden ornaments and porch furniture but we all had our suspicions.'

'Did Constable Derby find out who did it?' Alice-Miranda asked.

'No, but Mrs Parker's most treasured gnome – I think she called him Newton – began turning up on postcards sent from all around the country.'

Millie burst out laughing. 'That's hilarious. If I was Newton I'd have escaped too.'

Mrs Smith grinned. 'I shouldn't say so, but I think you're quite right about that.'

'I don't see why the carnival people should be blamed for things just because they're in town. I mean, it makes a perfect cover for anyone who wanted to get up to no good. They could just blame the travellers,' Alice-Miranda said decisively.

'I hear what you're saying, dear, but to be on the safe side, you just stay away and let them get on with preparing the village show,' Mrs Smith said sternly. 'Millie, would you like to come and get the sand-wiches while I make you some cordial?'

The girls ate their lunch and chatted with Mrs Smith about her plans for the next week's dinner menu.

'Now, what are you two doing this afternoon?' the cook asked as she cut two large brownies from the slab.

'We're going to see Mr Walt over at Chesterfield Downs,' Alice-Miranda replied.

'I'm heading over there later myself. I've got a lovely sponge and these brownies are for the lads' afternoon tea,' Mrs Smith explained. 'Then I might pop over to the hospital and see Evelyn for a while.'

'Could you take the card I've written for her, please?' Alice-Miranda asked. 'I feel awful. I wrote it on Monday evening and thought I'd put it into the post but then I saw it this morning underneath some papers on my desk. It must be old age – who knew that turning eight would have such an effect on my memory?'

Mrs Smith and Millie laughed.

'There's no hope for me then, is there?' Millie said. 'I'm almost eleven!'

'And what about me, dear – I shouldn't have any memory left at all given my positively ancient age.' The woman shook her head. 'Of course I'll take it for you, Alice-Miranda. I just hope I remember to give it to her.' She winked at Millie.

'I'll go and get it from the house. And thanks for lunch.' Alice-Miranda hopped down from her seat.

'I'll go get Chops and Bony,' Millie offered. 'Oh yeah, thanks for lunch,' she added before the two girls flew out the kitchen door.

Millie walked back up the hill towards the stables. She called out to Bony and Chops, who were happily grazing in the small holding paddock nearby. Bony's ears pricked up and he walked over to greet her. Much to her surprise, Chops also did as he was told.

'Hello boy.' Millie scratched his ear. 'You know I'd never really send you to the dog food factory, but let's just keep that between us.'

'He'd make a good few cans,' a voice spoke from behind her.

Millie jumped and spun around.

'Oh, Mr Boots,' she said. 'I didn't hear you come over.'

'What would you get for him?' the young man asked.

'Sorry, what do you mean?' Millie frowned.

'At the dog food factory?' he said. 'How much?'

'Oh, that was just a joke, to get him to behave a bit better,' Millie grinned.

'Reckon they'd give you a few quid.' Billy Boots stared at Chops, then turned his attention to Bonaparte. He ran his hand along the pony's sleek rump. 'Reckon you'd be worth a whole lot more, though.'

Bony jerked his head around and bared his teeth, then licked Billy's arm.

'Not again,' Billy slapped Bonaparte on the bottom and laughed. He led Bony and Chops through the gate.

'I'd better get going,' she said.

'Where to?' Billy asked.

'We're going over to Chesterfield Downs.'

'Chesterfield Downs?' Billy repeated. 'That's where Wally's gone, isn't it? He said it's a pretty nice place.'

'I've heard that too. But I've never been before. I just hope Wally hasn't had too many close encounters with Rockstar yet,' Millie grinned.

'Rockstar? You mean the champion racehorse? Does he live there?'

'Oh yes, he's the star of the stable,' Millie nodded.

'I bet he's worth a flipping fortune,' Billy exhaled.

'I suppose so. But he'll be worth a lot more when he wins the Queen's Cup,' said Millie. 'Aunty Gee hasn't ever won her own cup.'

'Who's Aunty Gee when she's at home?' Billy asked.

'That's Queen Georgiana, but she said that I could call her Aunty Gee,' Millie explained.

'How the heck do you know the Queen?' Billy scoffed. 'If you do, that is.'

'I really do. She's Alice-Miranda's mother's godmother and I've met her a few times now.'

'So Queen Georgiana owns Rockstar and *he* lives here in the village,' Billy said. He frowned and bit his lip.

'Yes, but his trainer Miss Pepper is laid up in hospital with a broken hip. I've never met Rockstar but everyone says that he and Miss Pepper have a special bond and he's completely mean to everyone else. I hope it doesn't affect his chances of winning. Anyway, I have to go,' Millie said. She'd just spotted

Alice-Miranda in the distance. The red-haired child led the two ponies away.

Something about Billy Boots gave Millie a strange feeling that she couldn't work out. She wondered if she'd been hanging around Alice-Miranda too long. He seemed nice enough and even Bonaparte liked him but he asked odd questions. Millie decided to talk to Alice-Miranda about her uneasiness as soon as possible.

Chapter 9

On the way to Chesterfield Downs, Millie told Alice-Miranda about her chat with Billy.

'There's just something about him. I really don't know what it is,' she finished, frowning.

Alice-Miranda nodded. 'I know a lot about strange feelings, Millie. Maybe you've caught it from me. I've found that there's usually an explanation for these things. Perhaps Mr Boots just needs someone to give him a chance.'

Millie nodded but she wasn't convinced.

'Come on.' Alice-Miranda clicked her tongue and Bonaparte began to canter. 'Or Mr Walt will think we're not coming.'

Miles and miles of hedgerows shielded much of Chesterfield Downs from view. The lane was bordered on the low side by a grove of alders, ash and beech trees, their leaves creating a pretty palette of green. Dappled sunlight lit the girls' way until they came to a pair of ancient limestone gateposts.

On the left a brass nameplate announced the property and on the right a small coat of arms and the letters HRH indicated that the farm was indeed owned by Her Royal Highness, Aunty Gee. An imposing set of iron gates stood open.

The brick-edged driveway seemed to go on forever, with emerald paddocks dotted with oak trees on either side and several horses grazing on the lush meadow grass.

As the girls rounded a bend in the road, a magnificent Georgian house came into view. It was three storeys through the centre with identical octagonal double-storey wings on either end. In the front of the property was a perfectly formed lake and a magnificent formal rose garden.

'Wow!' Millie exclaimed. 'What a beautiful house.'

'And garden. It's lovely,' Alice-Miranda agreed. 'I can't imagine why Aunty Gee doesn't come down here more often.'

'She probably has about ten houses just like this one,' Millie scoffed.

'I suppose so,' said Alice-Miranda. 'It does seem a little more than anyone needs. I wonder if she's ever thought to allow people who are down on their luck to stay here while they get back on their feet?'

'Are you thinking of Billy Boots?' Millie asked with a grin. 'Really? Aunty Gee is good fun but I can't imagine this place full of hobos.'

The girls spent another couple of minutes studying the house, and spotted a sign marked 'Stables' pointing towards the rear. They rode on and at the crest of the hill both girls gasped. The land flattened out and to the right an enormous stable complex dominated the landscape. It had a small clock tower in the centre and a row of dormer windows in the roof. A vast pair of timber doors stood open at the end. There was a small holding yard beside the building, and beyond yet another hedge was a full-sized racetrack. A whitewashed cottage sat amid a pretty garden just below the stables.

Millie's eyes were on stalks as she took it all in. 'What an amazing place.'

Alice-Miranda dismounted and pulled the reins over Bony's head. Millie did the same and then the two girls walked towards a hitching rail beside the stables and tied the ponies up side by side.

'Now, you two behave yourselves,' Alice-Miranda instructed.

There didn't seem to be anyone around. The girls walked towards the stables and peered inside.

Through the double row of stalls, at least a dozen down either side, the girls could just make out a group of people huddled at the other end of the building.

'Hello,' Alice-Miranda called out. 'May we come in?' She squinted as her eyes adjusted to the low light.

The group turned and looked at her.

'Hello Miss Alice-Miranda, Miss Millie,' Wally Whitstable called, beckoning them to enter.

The girls could hear a low murmuring as Wally explained to the others that these were the visitors he was expecting from Winchesterfield-Downsfordvale.

As she and Millie approached the group, Alice-Miranda noticed that they were all staring at something in the end stall.

'Good afternoon, ladies. I'd like to introduce you to Dick Wigglesworth, my boss,' said Wally.

A stocky man with thick grey caterpillar eyebrows turned and nodded at the girls. Alice-Miranda held out her hand, which the older fellow shook gently.

'It's lovely to meet you, Mr Wigglesworth. My name is Alice-Miranda Highton-Smith-Kennington-Jones,' she said with a smile.

Millie offered her hand too. 'And I'm Millie,' she said.

'Good afternoon, girls, and welcome to Chester-field Downs,' Dick Wigglesworth replied.

Wally introduced the rest of the group. There were four lads in total, all of whom Alice-Miranda insisted on greeting in the usual way.

'Well, you'd better get back to work, boys,' Dick Wigglesworth instructed. 'I don't think there's anything else for it.'

'Is that Rockstar in there?' Alice-Miranda asked, pointing at the stall behind the group.

'It certainly is. But at the moment he's anything but a rock star,' Dick replied.

The tiny child could barely see over the stable door. She looked around and saw a milk crate, which she collected and placed in front of it and then jumped up to get a better look.

'What's the matter with him?' Alice-Miranda asked as she hung over the door.

'Depressed, we think,' Dick replied. 'Ever since Evelyn went off to hospital.'

Millie jumped up beside Alice-Miranda. 'What about when he's outside?' she asked.

'That's part of the problem,' Dick informed her. 'No one's been able to *get* him outside.'

Alice-Miranda whispered to the stallion, 'Hello boy. Aren't you a handsome lad?'

The black beast ignored her. With his head in the corner and his rump turned out towards the onlookers, he responded by lifting his tail to blow some foul-smelling wind in their general direction.

'Pooh!' said Millie. 'That's disgusting.'

Alice-Miranda waved her hand in front of her nose. She turned to Dick and Wally. 'He doesn't look scary.'

'You don't want to open that door, Miss,' Wally said with a shudder. 'I made that mistake this morning and he almost took my head off. Makes your Bonaparte look like a kitten.'

'Does that mean he's not going to run in the Queen's Cup?' Millie asked.

Dick shook his head. 'He hasn't done track work for days. Unless there's a miracle soon, we're going to have to scratch him. I suppose there's always next year.'

Outside there was an explosion of whinnying. Rockstar's ears went back and he shifted his weight.

'Oh dear, it sounds like Chops and Bony are having a disagreement,' said Alice-Miranda. She jumped off the crate.

The whinnying escalated. Rockstar replied, softly at first but soon he was making as much noise as Bonaparte. The black stallion wheeled around and charged towards the stall door. Millie leapt down just as he threw his head over.

'I'd better see what's wrong with Bony,' said Alice-Miranda, and began to walk quickly towards the stable's entrance. She didn't run, as she knew that it might upset the other horses inside.

Suddenly the clip-clop of hooves on cobbles echoed through the building and Bonaparte appeared, running towards her.

His reins were dragging on the ground. Alice-Miranda tried in vain to grab them as he sped past her but she missed and he almost tripped himself up.

'How did you escape? Bonaparte Napoleon Highton-Smith-Kennington-Jones, you are the naughtiest pony I have ever known,' the girl called as she scurried after him.

The other horses in the stables all perked up, threw their heads over the stall doors and watched the pony's escapades.

By now Rockstar was pawing at the ground and whinnying at the top of his lungs. Bonaparte continued to reply.

Wally and Millie also grabbed at Bonaparte but he dodged both of them and ran straight for Rockstar's stall. He skidded to a halt and thrust his head up towards the door.

What happened next was completely unexpected.

Rockstar stopped his whinnying and so did Bony. The black stallion sniffed his small visitor. Bonaparte sniffed him back. Then Rockstar started rubbing his chin against Bony's nose.

'What's this then?' Dick Wigglesworth asked.

Alice-Miranda had rejoined the group and they all watched as Bonaparte and Rockstar engaged in some kind of equine conversation. There were neighs and whinnies and snorts and grunts.

'That's the strangest thing I've ever seen,' Dick whispered. 'He's never been one to get on with the other horses but he's completely taken by that fella of yours.'

Wally reached around and grabbed Bony's reins. 'Right, I think we'd better get you back outside and this time I'll put you in the holding yard.'

As Wally attempted to wheel Bonaparte around, the solid pony stood his ground and Rockstar reached out and nipped at the young lad's hair.

'Oi! You little monster,' he snapped, glaring at Bony.

'It wasn't him,' Millie said. 'It was him.' She pointed at Rockstar, who was grinding his teeth.

Wally made a second attempt at moving Bonaparte but the pony locked his knees and refused to budge. Alice-Miranda reached out and gave him a pat on the neck.

'Come along, Bonaparte, you can't stay here. Rockstar needs to rest,' she whispered in his ear before taking the reins from Wally.

In his stall, the champion began to paw at the ground.

'Mr Wigglesworth, do you think we could try something?' Wally asked.

'What are you thinking, lad?'

'I wondered if we might take them outside together,' Wally said.

'Oh no,' Dick replied. 'That doesn't sound like a good idea at all.'

'I reckon Miss Pepper would be well pleased if we could at least get him out of the stables. And she'd be over the moon if we could get him to run,' a lanky lad called Freddy piped up.

'So now you're an expert, are you, Freddy?' Dick challenged.

In his stall, Rockstar reared up. He looked as though he meant to break through the door.

'No, sir, but I think there's a good chance he could injure himself in there,' Freddy replied.

Dick Wigglesworth eyed the stallion. 'Steady on there, son,' he cooed.

'He's going to hurt himself, Mr Wigglesworth,' said Wally. His face was pale; he hated the thought of something happening to the horse.

'All right. Since you fellas know everything. Freddy, get his gear, will you?' Dick Wigglesworth instructed.

The boy looked at him and was motionless for a few seconds.

'Today, son, if it's not too much of a bother,' Dick huffed.

Freddy rushed off towards the tack room.

'But who's going to ride him?' Alice-Miranda asked, looking around the stables.

Freddy appeared, holding a bridle and tiny saddle, which he handed to Dick.

'Okay then, Wally, show us what you're made of.' The old man passed the bridle to Wally, who looked as if he'd swallowed a whale.

'I . . . I'm not going in there,' Wally quavered. 'You know him better than anyone.'

'You told me you wanted to work with race-horses. So here's your chance,' said Dick.

'Would you like me to bring Bonaparte in there with you while you get Rockstar ready?' Alice-Miranda asked Wally.

'What? And have two maniacs in together?' Wally gulped.

Dick Wigglesworth winked at her. 'Now you're thinking, young lady.'

'You shouldn't go in there, Miss Alice-Miranda,' Wally protested. 'It's not safe.'

'But you're going in there,' Alice-Miranda reasoned.

Wally's frown deepened. 'Exactly.'

Dick Wigglesworth opened the stall door and Alice-Miranda led Bonaparte into the box. The two horses stood nose to nose sniffing each other, before Rockstar began again to rub his face on Bonaparte's neck. It was the most extraordinary sight.

Wally edged his way inside and was surprised at how quickly and easily he got the bridle and saddle on Rockstar.

'Now, Alice-Miranda, I need you to lead Bonaparte back outside. Don't move too far away from this fellow,' Dick instructed.

Alice-Miranda did as she was asked and the two horses, Rockstar the seventeen-hand giant and Bonaparte the fourteen-hand pony, stood side by side – an odd couple indeed.

'You know they could almost be twins,' said Millie, laughing as she looked at the black pair. 'Except that Rockstar is gorgeous and Bonaparte is short and fat.'

'Get a helmet for Wally,' Dick barked at Freddy.

Wally shook his head. 'Oh, no! I'm not riding him, sir.'

'Well, then, we'll just have to put him away again,' Dick said. 'I can't do it. I've got a bad back and Freddy can't stay upright on a fence rail.'

The lad in question returned with a helmet, which he passed to Wally.

By now Rockstar was behaving like a perfect gentleman. Bony was too. Wally hesitated, then jammed the helmet on his head. Dick gave Wally a leg-up and he sat atop the giant beast.

'You too, miss,' said Dick, indicating that Alice-Miranda should mount Bony. 'I think you should go down to the track together and see what happens. But I don't imagine it will be much.'

Alice-Miranda urged Bonaparte forward. Wally did the same to Rockstar. Side by side the unlikely duo walked out of the stables and towards the track. There were nickers and neighs and lots of chatting between the two beasts. Millie, Dick and Freddy followed on foot.

'That's the strangest thing I've ever seen,' Freddy said. 'Only person who can handle him is Miss Pepper and the only jockey who can stay on him is Diego Dominguez.'

'Wally seems to be managing okay,' Millie commented as they watched Bony and Rockstar jogging towards the track.

'This way.' Dick Wigglesworth led Millie and Freddy through a gap in the hedge and they emerged on the side of the course.

Wally looked over at Alice-Miranda. 'I really don't know what's going to happen when we get on the track. If he goes off, we could both be in trouble.'

'Perhaps I should just try to keep up for a little while,' she suggested. 'Bony's no champion but we could give it our best, just to get Rockstar off and running.'

They reached the entrance to the racetrack and walked through.

'All right, are you ready?' Wally asked, taking a deep breath. He lowered his goggles and Alice-Miranda adjusted her helmet. 'Off you go first and I'll see if I can hold him.' Wally tightened his grip on the reins. He felt as if he'd swallowed a bucket of sand. The young lad licked his lips and told the butterflies in his stomach to keep still.

Alice-Miranda dug her heels into Bonaparte's flank and he took off.

'Come on boy, run fast and then you can have a treat,' she urged. At the mention of a treat Bony seemed to pick up the pace and his fast canter became a gallop. Behind them Walt Whitstable was doing his best to hold Rockstar, who was whinnying and dancing all over the place.

'All right, it's now or never.' Wally gave the

champion his head and he bolted towards Bonaparte. He was gaining on the pony and it didn't take long before he rounded the turn and raced for home, leaving Alice-Miranda in his mud-spattered wake.

'Go, Rockstar,' Millie shouted. 'Go, boy!'

'Whoo hoo!' Freddy pumped his fist into the air and clicked off his stopwatch. 'It's a good time too,' he said, staring at the numbers in front of him.

Dick Wigglesworth shook his head. 'I don't believe it.'

'There'll be no stopping him in the Queen's Cup now,' said Freddy with a smile.

Dick's shoulders slumped and he sighed loudly.

'Are you all right, Mr Wigglesworth?' Millie asked.

'Yes lass, fine, just fine,' he said slowly.

Rockstar snorted and sidestepped, then spun around as if looking for something. Alice-Miranda charged around the turn and when Bonaparte crossed the finish line, Rockstar greeted him with an ear-splitting whinny.

'That was amazing,' said Millie. She was standing on the lower fence rail with her arms slung over the top. Beside her, Freddy and Mr Wigglesworth were shaking their heads in disbelief.

'Well done, Mr Walt. That was incredible,' Alice-Miranda said to the young lad.

He was grinning broadly. 'I can't believe it. I stayed on him!' He reached down and patted Rockstar's neck.

Alice-Miranda patted her little fellow's neck too. 'Well done, Bonaparte. Good boy.'

Chapter 10

Ambrosia Headlington-Bear reached into the centre console and pushed the U-shaped lever. In a series of robotic movements, the roof of the shiny silver sports car folded itself neatly into a panel above the boot. A click and a pop signified the end of the process.

'That is sooooo cool,' Sloane gasped. 'I want a car just like this when I grow up.'

'It's not even that warm, Mummy. I don't see why you need to show off and put the roof down,' Jacinta fumed.

'Darling,' her mother cooed. 'What's the point in having a convertible if you don't get to use it? And Sloane seems to like it.'

'Sloane would.' Jacinta turned and glared at her friend in the back seat.

'Come on 'Cinta, don't be in a grump. We've had such a lovely day.' Ambrosia stuck out her lip, making sure that Sloane could see her in the rear-vision mirror.

Sloane clasped her hands over her mouth to smother a giggle.

'My name is Jacinta, Mother, with a J.' Jacinta folded her arms in front of her and stared through the passenger window, which she refused to put down just because the rest of the vehicle was open to the elements.

The unlikely threesome had been enjoying a particularly pleasant day until Ambrosia insisted that they stop at the village general store on their way back from seeing a movie in the city. It was the conversation that followed that had made Jacinta see red.

'If I'm going to spend some time in this place, the locals should really know that I'm here,' Ambrosia had informed the girls as the sports car sped into the village. 'I mean, once the paparazzi get hold of the location, the place is likely to be swarming with photographers.'

'Don't you mean, once your publicist lets it slip, Mummy, which I'm surprised she hasn't done already.'

'Oh, I couldn't have anyone taking photos of me outside the cottage before we fixed it up,' Ambrosia complained.

Jacinta rolled her eyes. 'I wouldn't know about that, seeing as you haven't taken me there yet – even though you've had it for a couple of months now.'

'Darling, you know tradesmen, they never finish anything on time,' Ambrosia said with a pout. 'Of course I want you to come and stay.'

'Mummy, you don't have to tell the paparazzi about the village. Wouldn't it be nice just to have some time for us – without anyone wanting to take your photograph?'

'Jacinta, you know that's not how the paps operate. We help each other. They sell photographs to magazines and I stay on top of everyone's invitation list,' Ambrosia informed her daughter.

At this revelation, Jacinta's mood had gone from fizz to fug.

Sloane had tried to help her friend find the positives. 'At least you get to see your mother during the term, Jacinta. I don't get to see my mother until the term break and then I have to go all the way to Barcelona.'

'But you told me yesterday that being back here is the best thing that has ever happened to you because now you don't have to put up with your mother and her whining,' Jacinta said.

'I didn't mean it exactly like that. It's complicated,' Sloane snapped back.

'Yes and so is this.' Jacinta was beginning to wonder if her mother renting the cottage was a good idea after all. She had been stupid to get her hopes up and think that things had really changed between the two of them.

Ambrosia parked the car outside the village store and asked the girls if they wanted an ice-cream. Jacinta was less than enthusiastic but Sloane was keen and the trio hopped out of the vehicle.

A bell tinkled above the shop door as the group entered. The proprietor, Herman Munz, was standing behind the counter watching an ancient television set on the end of the bench.

'Hello,' Ambrosia smiled.

'Hello, may I help you vith somethink?' Herman asked.

'The girls are going to get some ice-creams but I just wanted to say hello. I've recently got a little place in the village. Wisteria Cottage.' Ambrosia batted her long lashes.

Herman Munz had turned his attention back to the television and seemed engrossed in the drama on the screen.

Ambrosia tried again. 'So I imagine that *you'll* be delivering my groceries.'

'No, that vill be my boy, Otto,' said Herman, still focused on the set.

Ambrosia rolled her eyes, then turned around and stared at the magazine rack behind her.

'Oh, look at that,' she cooed. 'Fancy.'

Herman ignored her. Jacinta and Sloane were hovering over the freezer at the back of the store deciding which ice-creams they would have.

'Goodness, that's amazing,' Ambrosia laughed to herself. It was rather forced but it did the trick.

Herman Munz glanced at her. She was an attractive woman, and well-dressed too. 'Vot are you looking at?' he asked.

Ambrosia spun on her towering heels and threw

a copy of the latest *Gloss and Goss* down in front of him.

Herman stared at the page, then back at Ambrosia and shrugged.

'Can't you see?' she asked.

Herman shook his head. 'I don't know vot I am supposed to be seeing.'

'It's me!' Ambrosia's high-pitched shriek caused the man to jump. She pointed a perfectly manicured finger at a photograph of herself dressed in a stunning gold gown. 'I'm at the FFATAS.' She ran her left hand through her brunette tresses.

'Who is farters?' Herman asked blankly.

'Are you joking?' Ambrosia stared at the man in disbelief. 'Everyone knows about the FFATAS.'

'Not me.' Herman's blue eyes stared vacantly at the picture. 'But is nice frock. You look good.'

'For your information, Mr . . .' Ambrosia sniffed. Jacinta and Sloane had joined her at the counter and placed their ice-creams on the bench.

'It's Mr Munz, Mummy,' Jacinta said. So much for her mother introducing herself, she thought.

'For your information, Mr Munz, the FFATAS are the Foreign Film and Television Awards.'

'Are you actress?' he asked. 'Because I don't know you.'

Ambrosia shook her head.

'Are you director?'

Ambrosia shook her head again.

'Writer? Camera operator, sound person?' Herman Munz was drawing a blank.

'Of course not.' Ambrosia's mouth turned down slightly in a frown, although the rest of her face didn't move.

'Then you are married to one?'

'No,' Ambrosia scowled.

'Then why you go to FFATAS and get photograph in magazine?' Herman asked.

'Because I'm Ambrosia Headlington-Bear, that's why.' Ambrosia opened her purse and pulled out a large note, which she pushed angrily across the counter.

'Sorry, I not know who that is.' Herman rang up the amount for the ice-creams and magazine and began to count out Ambrosia's change.

Ambrosia pushed the magazine towards him. 'I'm not buying that. I've already got three copies.'

Herman pointed at a sign behind the counter. 'You read magazine, you buy magazine.'

The hulky man pushed the volume back towards Ambrosia.

'Hmph.' She turned and strode out of the store, leaving Jacinta and Sloane in her wake.

'I'm sorry, Mr Munz,' Jacinta apologised, 'but you've just had the pleasure of meeting my mother.'

'Vos no pleasure, Miss Jacinta. But you are not like her,' he said and grinned at the blonde girl.

Jacinta and Sloane picked up their ice-creams and peeled off the wrappers, depositing the papers in the bin outside the shop.

Ambrosia was sitting in the car, red-faced and flicking her fingernails.

'You'd better hurry up and eat those before you get in,' she called. Her lower lip quivered. 'I want to go home and I have to get you back to school.'

Jacinta couldn't believe her ears. She threw the rest of the ice-cream in the bin.

'But I thought we were staying out with you, Mummy?' She opened the passenger door and pulled the back seat forward for Sloane to wedge herself in.

'I can't stay down tonight. I have a ball back in town. Your father is coming in from overseas and he insisted I go with him,' Ambrosia explained. 'I think he's got something for me. He was being very mysterious on the telephone. I rather hope it's that gorgeous diamond necklace I've had my eye on.

It would be just perfect with the pink Chanel gown I'm planning to wear.'

'I should have guessed there would be something more important than me. I don't think I'm ever going to see Wisteria Cottage,' Jacinta complained, folding her arms in front of her, 'let alone stay there.'

'Of course you're the most important thing, darling. It's just that Daddy really wants to see me, and we haven't spent any time together for ages. You know him; his whole life is just work, work, and more work. Anyway, I'm sure you could con that dowdy old housemistress into taking you to the cottage if you're that desperate to have a look. There's a key under the flowerpot at the back door. Heavens knows the place is nothing special. It needs a load of work. Besides, I'll be back again in a week or two.' Ambrosia hit the start button beside the steering wheel. The engine purred like a lion. She glanced around to see if anyone was watching, then put her foot to the accelerator and roared off down the street.

Chapter 11

'I can't believe you're going to leave him here,' Millie said as she and Alice-Miranda left the stable block.

'It's the best thing for Rockstar,' said Alice-Miranda. 'He and Bony seem to have a connection, and if it means that Mr Wigglesworth can train Rockstar to run in the Queen's Cup, then it's the least I can do. Imagine how pleased Aunty Gee would be if Rockstar won! We can come over tomorrow to visit. Maybe they'll have had a fight by then and I'll be able to take Bony home,' she finished with a little smile.

'But we can't train for the show,' Millie said sulkily.

'If Bonaparte gets a workout like that every day, he'll be fitter than ever for the show. Maybe I could ask someone to drive me over after school to see him during the week,' Alice-Miranda suggested.

'I suppose so,' Millie said with a frown. 'Anyway, you're going to have to double back with me on Chops this afternoon and I can't guarantee it will be the best riding experience of your life.'

'I will be honoured to accept a lift.' Alice-Miranda curtsied.

After witnessing Rockstar's behaviour on the track, Alice-Miranda had started to wonder. She'd heard about racehorses sometimes having companion ponies but she'd never seen anything like it before.

Wally had joked that he'd come to Chesterfield Downs to get away from Bony the menace, but he thought it was awfully kind of Alice-Miranda to let him stay there for Rockstar's sake.

The only person who hadn't seemed terribly excited about having Bony was Mr Wigglesworth, but Alice-Miranda had insisted. When she'd pointed out that Aunty Gee would be pleased to know that Rockstar was at least out training again, he seemed to change his mind. She thought Miss Pepper would be thrilled too.

Alice-Miranda had kissed Bonaparte goodbye and said that she would come and see how he was getting on tomorrow. He had ignored her completely, which was not unusual.

Now, outside in the sunshine, the two girls were chatting about the events they planned to enter in the show when they spied Mrs Smith's car trundling towards them.

'Hello,' Alice-Miranda called out as the cook turned off the ignition and hopped out.

'Hello girls,' Mrs Smith said with a wave. From inside the car she retrieved a sizable biscuit tin and a huge plate containing an equally huge strawberry sponge cake.

Alice-Miranda took the tin and Millie offered to help carry the cake but Mrs Smith just asked that she close the car door.

'How was your ride?' the older woman asked.

'Eventful,' Millie replied.

'And how's Wally settling in?' Mrs Smith motioned for Millie to open the gate that led to the whitewashed cottage in front of the stables.

'He's amazing,' Alice-Miranda said, her eyes wide.

'Amazing?' Doreen frowned at Alice-Miranda. 'Really? I'm looking forward to hearing what he's done to earn such high praise on his first day. Now, Mr Wigglesworth said I should leave these at the cottage,' said Mrs Smith.

On hearing the visitors' approach, Evelyn Pepper's faithful hound Keith raised his head and began to howl.

'Hello there boy.' Alice-Miranda reached down and gave the basset a pat on the head. He reciprocated by sniffing her hand.

Mrs Smith motioned for Millie to open the back door and the girls followed her inside.

The country kitchen was warm and inviting with a fire burning in the giant AGA stove.

Doreen placed the cake on the pine table in the centre of the room and Alice-Miranda handed her the tin of brownies.

The screen door opened and Dick Wigglesworth entered the kitchen.

'Hello Doreen. This is marvellous,' he said, spying the sponge cake on the table. He planted a kiss on her cheek. 'With Evelyn away it feels like we're running on half-steam. Place just isn't the same without her. But all this food has been wonderful.

The lads just about inhaled those chicken sandwiches you made yesterday.'

'It's no trouble at all. I'm quite used to feeding the masses and I'm glad it's a help to Ev.'

'You're a good friend, Doreen,' Dick said.

'And how's Wally settling in?' Mrs Smith asked.

'The lad's doing all right,' Dick replied.

'All right!' Millie exclaimed. 'I think he's doing better than all right. He rode Rockstar down on the track.'

'Rockstar!' Doreen gasped. 'But I thought the only one who could ever get near him was Evelyn.'

'That's what we were going to tell you, Mrs Smith,' Alice-Miranda began. 'Rockstar has made friends with Bony, so I'm going to leave him here for a few days so that Mr Walt can ride track work and then Rockstar will still have a chance at winning the Queen's Cup.'

'Of course he's going to win,' Millie nodded.

'Don't get ahead of yourselves there, girls. It was just one run and who knows how the young upstart will wake up in the morning. I think he's only a very slim chance of running in the cup,' Dick Wigglesworth replied as he filled the kettle and placed it on the stovetop.

'How are you getting back to school, dear?' Mrs Smith asked Alice-Miranda.

'Alice-Miranda's going to double with me on Chops,' Millie said.

'Oh, that doesn't sound very comfortable,' said Mrs Smith. 'Are you sure you wouldn't rather come back with me? Millie, perhaps you can leave Chops here with Bony and his friends until tomorrow? I can drop you off at school before I go to see Evelyn at the hospital. It's no trouble.'

Millie shrugged. 'I suppose we could do that – if there's a spare stall in the stables?'

Dick Wigglesworth nodded. 'I'm sure we can find a spot for him, Millie, but I suggest you both come back in the morning. I think Bony will be right to go home tomorrow.'

Wally Whitstable arrived at the back door with Freddy and another couple of the lads. 'Hello Mrs Smith,' the young man greeted the older woman.

'What about you, then? Wait until I tell Charlie about your heroics riding Rockstar,' Mrs Smith exclaimed as she gave Wally a hug.

'It wasn't planned, Mrs Smith, I can tell you that. I only got on him 'cos of this little one.' He nodded towards Alice-Miranda.

'You were perfect, Mr Walt,' she said, grinning at him.

'Surprised myself a bit,' Wally said. 'Didn't think I'd ever ride anything half as good as him. I didn't even want to think about him being owned by Her Majesty, or what he'll be worth when he's finished on the track.'

'What do you mean?' Millie asked.

'Stallions like him are worth a fortune, Miss Millie, because once they stop racing they can father lots of babies who might also turn out to be champions,' Wally explained.

'Or donkeys,' said Dick Wigglesworth with raised eyebrows. 'They don't always sire good offspring, but usually you'd expect a few decent runners out of them.'

'Of course,' Millie replied.

Mrs Smith suggested that Alice-Miranda and Millie head off and put Chops away and she'd meet them outside in a few minutes.

The girls bade farewell to the lads and Mr Wigglesworth and headed off to the stables.

With Chops safely away for the night, Alice-Miranda, Millie and Mrs Smith set off in the cook's positively ancient Mini. At the bottom of the driveway something in the trees opposite caught Alice-Miranda's attention.

'There's someone over there,' she said, pointing towards the slope.

'I can't see anyone, dear,' the cook replied, squinting. 'But that doesn't count for much these days.'

Alice-Miranda could have sworn it was a child.

Millie spotted a movement too. 'You're right. Oh,' she groaned. 'It's that girl from the carnival.'

'You mean Fern?' Alice-Miranda said. 'Could you stop the car please, Mrs Smith?'

'Now, why would I want to do that, young lady?' Doreen Smith kept her foot on the accelerator and the vehicle puttered along the laneway.

'I just thought I should talk to her,' Alice-Miranda replied, 'and ask if she's okay.'

'I think you should leave well enough alone,' Mrs Smith said firmly.

Alice-Miranda leaned around to look back. The girl was now standing on the edge of the road, staring at them.

Millie looked around too. 'She's a bit odd. Her eyes are like a cat's.'

But Alice-Miranda didn't feel the same way. Something about the carnival girl and her brother gave her a strange feeling and she was eager to find out why.

As Mrs Smith reached the main road the girls were surprised to see Ambrosia Headlington-Bear's sports car speeding towards them. With the roof down and the wind in her hair, Ambrosia was singing along with the radio and clearly feeling quite pleased with herself.

'I wonder where Jacinta and Sloane are,' Millie asked as the car roared past. 'I thought they were staying with her tonight.'

Alice-Miranda grimaced. 'It doesn't look that way.'

Although Jacinta hadn't exactly said so, Alice-Miranda had guessed that her friend was looking forward to the weekend with her mother very much. The mere fact that she had asked to wear the dress Ambrosia had sent her was indication enough. And now Ambrosia was speeding out of the village without any sign of Jacinta or Sloane. Alice-Miranda's tummy knotted. Poor Jacinta.

Millie had a similar thought. 'If her mother's done something to upset her, Jacinta will be in a right foul mood. I'm glad she's sharing with Sloane.'

'Millie,' Alice-Miranda scolded her friend. 'I have a feeling Jacinta might need all of us to cheer her up.'

Doreen Smith glanced at her tiny charge sitting beside her in the passenger seat. 'Why don't I make Jacinta's favourite dessert tonight?' she said.

'Oh, Mrs Smith, I think that's a wonderful idea,' Alice-Miranda replied. 'I think its cherry cheesecake.'

The woman nodded. 'Consider it done.'

Chapter 12

Myrtle Parker arrived home from her errands and stared sadly at the jungle of weeds growing among the roses in the front garden. She was tired of living a widow's life, having lost her beloved Reginald years ago. Except Reginald wasn't dead, he was just asleep in the front sitting room.

It had happened one evening when Evelyn was on her way home from a Show Society meeting. She had left Reginald with his favourite dinner, curried sausages, and a list of jobs that needed doing before she got back. Myrtle arrived at the front door to find him up a ladder on the roof in the dark, clearing out the gutters. She hadn't meant to startle the silly man, but startled he was and he slipped right off the edge. Myrtle discovered him lying on the driveway in an odd position. His injuries didn't appear to be life threatening at the time – a broken leg and a gash on the forehead – but while he was in hospital something terribly strange happened.

Myrtle visited every day, telling him how much she needed him and bringing in an ever-growing list of chores that would need to be attended to as soon as he was out of hospital. According to one of the nurses, Reginald was reading the list one morning when his eyes began to get heavy. She asked him if he was all right and the poor man just said that he was tired – exhausted, really. He closed his eyes and had been asleep ever since. That was three years ago.

Test after test said that there was plenty of activity going on in his brain and his body seemed to have recovered from the injuries. No one could work it out. There was some nasty talk around the village that Myrtle had driven him to it – the poor man, never getting a minute's rest. But of course that wasn't true. Myrtle was a stickler for eight hours sleep a night, not a minute more, not a minute less.

The doctors said that he should make a full recovery but after six months they simply gave up, saying they couldn't understand it. One of the physicians said that it was as if he didn't want to wake up. Every now and then, usually on the days that Myrtle was too busy to visit him, a smile would settle on the man's face.

Myrtle trekked back and forth to the hospital in Downsfordvale. The whole arrangement was highly problematic, particularly in the lead-up to showtime, when Myrtle was always busier than an ants' nest before a summer storm.

The doctors wondered if Reginald might do better in his own surroundings. So Myrtle took him home and set him up in the sitting room as the bedrooms were far too small to accommodate the required equipment. She found this a terrible inconvenience when it came to entertaining. Afternoon tea parties were never the same again as the ladies were forced to spy each other over the top of the bedclothes. On a couple of occasions Myrtle thought that all the noise her friends made might wake him up, but if anything, their presence seemed to send him into an even deeper sleep.

Home care was expensive too but Reginald had been a sensible man and his life insurance policy covered the cost of a live-in nurse, although they were usually unreliable young things and Myrtle frequently found herself having to interview new staff.

So, despite the fact that Reginald lived and breathed, Myrtle considered herself as much a widow as any other in the village.

With the whole afternoon on her hands, she decided to give the sitting room some special attention. The new nurse, a stout woman called Raylene, had ducked out to the pharmacy. If the past couple of weeks were any indication, she'd be gone at least a couple of hours. The woman seemed to find any number of things to do that kept her away from the house.

Myrtle grabbed her apron from the pantry and went into the utility room to retrieve her antiquated upright vacuum cleaner. Perhaps the sounds and smells of good cleaning would rouse Reginald from his slumber. She'd even tried to polish his head one day in the hope that it might wake him. He had just sneezed and coughed a little, then settled back to his usual state of inertia.

Myrtle plugged the ancient beast into the wall socket and set forth hoovering every inch of the room, including the settee.

Over the din, she thought she heard a chime. Myrtle flicked off the switch and pushed the handle back to the vertical position. She wondered who might be calling on her – most of her friends only ever came when there was a committee meeting. The village folk were well aware of the difficulty of her having Reginald in the sitting room.

Myrtle opened the front door. There was no one there. She peered outside and down the path to the street but couldn't see anyone. She decided that she must have been hearing things, closed the door and went back to her hoovering. Not a minute after the machine had whirred back to life, the bell went again.

'Goodness me.' Myrtle flicked the switch off again. 'I'll be right there,' she called and didn't dally getting to the hallway.

'Hello?' She reefed opened the front door. Her eyes darted around the yard. 'Show yourself.'

Myrtle waited a moment and then slammed the door. She stomped back to the vacuum and began for the third time. But something told her that this game was not over. She snapped off the whirring appliance and hurried to the front door, just as the bell rang.

'Gotcha!' Myrtle flung open the door expecting to see some or other scruffy child thinking themselves very funny for playing tricks on an old woman. But that wasn't what she observed at all.

'Oh my goodness! Newton?' she gulped. 'Is it really you? Have you come home to Mother?'

Newton was silent. Sitting beside him was a folded piece of paper. Myrtle picked it up, opened it and read:

I'm sorry that I ran away last year but I wanted some adventures. Please don't be mad at me. I've had the best time ever and I've seen loads of places and met interesting people but I thought it was time to come home again.

Myrtle looked down at the concrete statue in front of her.

'Oh Newton, I'm so glad that you're back. I've missed you terribly.' Tears pooled in the old woman's eyes. 'It hasn't been the same without you. No one to talk to about Reginald, no one who under-stands what it's like for me with him in there taking up all that space in the sitting room. I'm sorry that I left you outside. I won't make that mistake ever again.'

Myrtle picked up the gnome and hugged it as if her very life depended on it. She peered into the garden to see if there was anyone lurking about.

'I know it was you lot from the carnival. It's a year almost to the day that my Newton went missing,' she called into the open air. 'I have a good mind to have you all locked up.'

She turned and walked back inside, wondering if the carnival people were already back in town and wishing that the show committee would heed her advice and hold the event without those ghastly rides and sideshows.

'Reginald, Reginald, you're never going to believe who's come home.' Myrtle Parker carried the gnome into the sitting room and put him down on the end of her husband's bed. 'Now, why don't you come back to me too?' she whispered at the man under the covers. 'I've got some very nice jobs for you to do.'

Chapter 13

When Alice-Miranda and Millie returned to Grimthorpe House, a tense mood hung over the building.

They found Sloane first, sitting in the common room thumbing through a magazine. When Sloane explained what had happened with Ambrosia and why she and Jacinta weren't staying out for the night as planned, Alice-Miranda decided to go and find Jacinta at once and try to cheer her up. Millie preferred to keep Sloane company for a little while.

She still had vivid memories of Jacinta's reign as the school's second best tantrum thrower.

Alice-Miranda made her way along the hallway to Jacinta's room and knocked on the door.

'Go away! I'm not coming out and whoever you are, you're not coming in,' Jacinta bellowed.

'Jacinta, it's me, Alice-Miranda,' she called as she knocked again.

'I still don't want to talk to you!' Jacinta shouted back.

'You might feel better if you talk to someone,' said Alice-Miranda. She pushed open the door and found Jacinta sitting on the floor. Unlike the first time Alice-Miranda had met her months before, she was not squealing with the might of ten elephants, but she *was* busy tearing a magazine to shreds.

Alice-Miranda was shocked. 'Jacinta, is that a picture of your mother?'

'So what if it is! It's just a stupid magazine and she'll be in a million more,' Jacinta spat.

Alice-Miranda sat cross-legged on the floor opposite her friend. 'I gather your day didn't turn out quite the way you'd hoped it would,' she said gently.

Jacinta's bottom lip began to tremble. 'She hasn't changed. You remember all that fussing about me on the ship when she thought I'd been kidnapped? Saying that she would spend more time with me? It was all a lie. She doesn't care about me. You know why she couldn't stay? She has to go to a ball. A ball! As if she hasn't been to a million balls before!'

A tear spilled onto Jacinta's cheek and trickled to the edge of her chin.

'Oh Jacinta, I'm sure that your mother loves you. She's just learning how to show it.' Alice-Miranda reached out and touched Jacinta's arm. 'Don't you remember that she hadn't been to see you in almost a year until you saw her on the ship?'

Jacinta had begun to cry properly. Big shuddery sobs, with real salty tears.

'Was today mostly okay?' Alice-Miranda asked her friend.

Jacinta looked up at her. Her blue eyes glistened, the colour of wet sapphires.

She nodded slowly.

'You've just got to give it time,' Alice-Miranda assured her. 'She's had a lot of years of doing whatever she's wanted, whenever she's wanted. I think some-times grown-ups behave much more like children than most children ever do.'

Jacinta brushed the moisture from her eyes. 'You

know, when she sent me this dress, I actually thought that maybe she was starting to get me. It's much more my style and not like all those other outfits she's sent before that made me look like a mini Ambrosia. And today we *did* have a good time, until she started talking about the paparazzi. It's like she can't help herself and she just has to have her picture taken all the time. I don't get it. When I make it to the Olympics, it will be because I've used every ounce of talent I've got and worked really hard to be the best I can be,' Jacinta explained. 'I'd hate to be famous just because I look a certain way. That's so stupid.'

Alice-Miranda couldn't agree more but she thought it was probably best not to comment. She did have a mind to call Ambrosia, though, and tell her how disappointed Jacinta was about their weekend being cut short.

Instead, Alice-Miranda said, 'Come on, Jacinta, let's get this cleaned up.' She began to pick up the paper.

Jacinta managed a small smile. 'I must look pretty stupid.'

'Of course not. I won't tell anyone.' Alice-Miranda leaned forward and gave Jacinta a hug. 'Why don't you go and wash your face and then we can play a game before dinner. I heard Mrs Smith is making cherry cheesecake for dessert.'

'Cherry cheesecake. She hardly ever makes that.' Jacinta wondered if somehow Alice-Miranda had been responsible for the dessert.

'I know. We've had a bit of an adventure today,' Alice-Miranda said as she offered her hand to help Jacinta up.

'How do you mean?' Jacinta asked. 'And what happened to your forehead?'

'Let's get cleaned up and then Millie and I will tell you all about it.'

That evening, Alice-Miranda, Millie and Sloane worked hard to cheer Jacinta up. After dinner – a delicious lasagne and the special cherry cheese-cake for dessert – the girls had been allowed to watch a movie and eat popcorn until bedtime. They let Jacinta choose and as usual ended up watching *London Calling* starring Lawrence Ridley for the umpteenth time. At least Jacinta's mood improved.

'Oh, he's so gorgeous,' she swooned a dozen

times. 'Your Aunt Charlotte is the luckiest woman in the world to be married to him.'

The other girls laughed.

'What about Lucas?' said Sloane. 'He's not exactly hideous, either.'

'No, he's adorable too,' Jacinta replied dreamily.

'I thought I might ask him to go to the show with me,' Sloane said blithely.

Alice-Miranda and Millie gulped in unison.

'I don't think that's a good idea,' said Millie.

Alice-Miranda shook her head. Jacinta was in a much better mood but if she thought Sloane was about to start flirting with Lucas, things were likely to get very ugly.

Jacinta stared at Sloane. 'There's no point,' she said sharply, 'because he's already asked me.'

Sloane pulled a face. 'I was just kidding. As if I'd ever ask. Boys are stinky little creatures, even if some of them are nice to look at.'

Alice-Miranda and Millie giggled.

'Your brother's lovely,' Alice-Miranda added.

'Sep? No, he's not. He's completely disgusting. You've never been in his room after he's eaten Mexican food.' Sloane held her fingers to her nose.

The girls went off to bed in high spirits.

Chapter 14

'Fern and Tarquin sitting in a tree, K-I-S-S-I-N-G. First comes love, then comes marriage, then comes Fern with a baby's carriage,' the mousy child chanted at the top of her lungs.

'Get lost, Ivy! He's my brother and you're disgusting,' Fern yelled.

Ivy stuck out her tongue. 'Are you gonna make me?' she challenged.

'I'm gonna get Pete onto you if you don't shut your filthy little mouth,' Fern threatened.

'Well, I'll tell Alf and then he'll kick you out and you'll have nowhere to live,' said the smaller girl, screwing up her face. 'Alf doesn't have to let you stay, you know. Not any more. He's the boss now.'

Fern eyeballed her. 'Who says?'

'My mum and she knows everything,' said Ivy.

'Your mum wouldn't know her right arm from her rear end!' Fern leapt down from the low branch where she'd been sitting and Ivy dashed away to join some of the other children, who were kicking their scuffed football across the open field.

When Alf had first arrived at the camp a couple of years back, sniffing around for work, some of the older blokes had been suspicious of him. But they were down a couple of men and even though Alf sounded like he gargled gravel for breakfast, he was a gentle giant – at least, that's what they'd all thought. Best of all, he made people laugh. It wasn't long before everyone loved him. Especially Gina, Fern and Tarquin's mother. Alf had married Gina and moved into the big van. Gina said that he would look after them and keep the carnival running properly until it was time for their older brother to take over. But then everything changed, especially Alf.

Fern nursed her throbbing arm. She had administered her own first aid, some ice in a plastic bag, then she'd wrapped it in an old crepe bandage she'd found in the caravan. But it hurt, worse than anything she'd felt before. She removed the bandage to have a look. Her wrist was swollen and it had started to bruise – maybe there was a broken bone. But it would just have to get better on its own. Alf wouldn't pay for her to see a doctor.

She could see her brother sitting in the grass at the edge of the field, near the willows. She reapplied the bandage, then walked over to him.

'Hey Tarq, I got this for you.' Fern reached into her pocket and pulled out a new badge. 'I found it in the village.'

Tarquin's amber eyes shone like new moons as he stared at the silver pin.

He reached out and took it, and immediately placed it on the ground beside the one from Chicken Charlie's.

'It's twinkly,' he said. 'I like it.'

Then he looked at Fern in a way she couldn't ever remember him looking before.

'I want Mum, Fern,' Tarquin said. 'And Liam.'

'I want them back too,' Fern said. 'But I don't know where Liam is and Mum's not coming back. Remember? She's gone to heaven.'

'With Marty?' Tarquin looked at his sister closely.

She sighed. 'Yeah, with Marty.'

If her little brother wanted to believe that their mother was in heaven with a skinny field mouse, then let him think that.

'Marty died,' Tarquin said.

'Yes, Marty died,' Fern repeated. She'd been glad about that, in a way. Tarquin's collections were hard enough to deal with when they weren't alive. There were rocks and coins and shiny pieces of paper and she wasn't ever allowed to throw anything away. The badges were a relatively new obsession. When Tarquin had found the mouse in the kitchen cupboard she had dreaded how they could cope with a collection of furry rodents. But then Marty the mouse had been dead the next morning and Tarquin had lost interest.

Fern had buried Marty in the field next to the racetrack at Cossington Park. Their mother was buried in the cemetery in the village at Winchesterfield. When you lived with the carnival you couldn't be fussy about where you left your dead. It was usually wherever the carnival was pulled in and it just so happened that almost a year ago their mother had taken her last breaths on the same flat piece of ground where the troupe had now set up their temporary home.

Fern had known that her mother was sick, but she had always said that she'd get better. That she wouldn't leave them. But she'd lied, because she'd died anyway and then Liam left too. Fern had no idea where he was or if he was all right, but he shouldn't have done what he did. Alf said that he had no choice but to tell him to go – at least that's what everyone said.

That afternoon, Fern had taken a long walk across the fields and around the village, but not to the cemetery. She wanted to go there but her legs wouldn't walk in that direction. And she'd seen that girl again, the one with the pony, and her red-haired friend. They were with an old lady driving out of the Queen's racing stables.

Fern had thought she looked the type. Stuck up little princess.

But there was no point complaining. Life was what it was. Some people had it easy and some didn't, but that made Fern all the more determined. Keeping up with school when you moved every month or less wasn't easy, but Fern's mother had enrolled her so that she could take her lessons via correspondence.

They'd had a teacher with them for a while but then Ivy's mother, Maude, had accused the young woman of being lazy when Ivy's brother Stephen failed some stupid scholarship test and the girl upped and left. Fern had loved working with the teacher. She wasn't lazy. Stephen, on the other hand, was no Einstein. After that, they hadn't been able to find a replacement. Fern's mother was smart and she could always help her daughter with her studies but since she'd been gone Fern had to slog twice as hard to work things out on her own. Sometimes another one of the carnival mums, Mrs Kessler, would have a look over her writing, and Mr Kessler was good with numbers but with four children of their own to look after, they didn't have much time.

In some ways Fern and Tarquin were the envy of the rest of the carnival because they had more space than anyone. Their mother had saved every penny she earned for years to buy the second-hand caravan they called home. While it was far from new, it was spotless. It was a little like a time machine, a perfectly preserved house on wheels from at least thirty years before. But it didn't feel much like home any more.

Fern had dreams – big dreams to leave the carnival and go to university. She wanted to become a doctor and then she'd make enough money to look after Tarquin properly. They could have a house – a proper house that you couldn't hitch up to the back of a truck – and there would be a garden too. More than anything, people would respect her; Fern knew that doctors were important. When you were in the carnival no one gave you any respect. Usually they were just afraid of you. She wondered what it would be like to have people want to be friends, instead of going out of their way to walk on the other side of the street just so they didn't have to make eye contact.

But carnival life wasn't all bad. You could go on the rides anytime you liked without paying, and Fern had seen more of the country than most people would ever see in their whole life. But still she wondered what it would be like to go to the same school every day and have the same friends. For now it was just her and Tarquin.

'Fern!' a voice growled from over by their caravan. 'I'm not waiting until midnight for my supper so you'd better get your sorry self home and start cooking.'

Fern flinched. She was thankful it was her left wrist that was damaged and not her right, but cutting up the vegetables was still going to be a challenge. Perhaps she'd just make something with rice tonight. At least Alf wasn't all that fussy about what she cooked, as long as there was a meal on the table.

'Tarquin,' she called to her brother. 'Come and help me with dinner.' She knew that 'help' meant he would just sit at the kitchen table and lay out his badges but she preferred his company to being on her own.

Tarquin looked up from his collection. He counted the badges one by one and placed them back into the drawstring bag, then he stood up beside her. Fern slipped her right hand into Tarquin's. He flinched.

'It's okay, Tarq,' she said. 'It's okay.' Together they walked home.

Chapter 15

On Sunday morning after breakfast, Alice-Miranda and Millie asked Mrs Howard if she had time to take them over to Chesterfield Downs to check on Bony and Chops. The girls decided they could ride home together on Chops if it looked like Bonaparte should stay longer.

'Oh, I am sorry, dears, but I have a show committee meeting this morning. If I know Myrtle Parker, I'll be given a list of extra jobs as long as my arm if I'm late. And I'm afraid that Charlie and Doreen will be joining me so there's no point asking them either,' Mrs Howard explained.

'Maybe we could go and see if Stumps is up for a ride. We could double over together and then you could ride him back. But just remember: don't mention the "h" word,' Millie said with a giggle.

Alice-Miranda nodded. 'That sounds like a good idea.'

The 'h' word Millie was referring to was *home*. Stumps was notorious for bolting home if anyone mentioned the word. Poor Sloane had found out the hard way after he'd taken off at a cracking pace the first and only time she'd been out riding with the girls.

Alice-Miranda and Millie headed off to the stables to find Stumps. They waved goodbye to Sloane and Jacinta, who had decided to walk over to Caledonia Manor to visit Sloane's step-granny Henrietta and Miss Hephzibah.

'Hello,' Alice-Miranda called as they entered the cool brick stable block. It seemed strange not to be greeted by Bony and Chops. Susannah's pony Buttercup whinnied hello, but Stumps was nowhere to be seen.

'I wonder where he is,' said Millie after they'd checked all of the stalls.

'Maybe he's been turned out already,' Alice-Miranda replied.

'Then we have no hope of taking him,' said Millie. 'Once he's in the paddock for the day he'll do anything to avoid being caught, the lazy little monster.'

'We might just have to walk to Chesterfield Downs,' Alice-Miranda suggested.

'But it's so far,' Millie groaned. 'And I'm tired already.'

'Chesterfield Downs, you say?' Billy Boots appeared behind the girls.

Millie just about leapt into the rafters and Alice-Miranda jumped too.

'Bit nervy, are we?' he asked.

'Oh, hello Mr Boots. We didn't hear you come in,' said Alice-Miranda, smiling at the young man.

'You're like a phantom,' Millie added, remembering how he had sneaked up on her the day before when she was collecting Bony and Chops from the paddock.

'I like that. A phantom,' Billy said with a wink.

'Is Stumps outside?' Millie asked.

'Sure is. I turned the little plodder out half an hour ago. He's got no go in him until he sees that grass and then you'd think someone had shoved a firecracker up his . . .'

Charlie Weatherly appeared at the entrance to the stables. 'Good morning all,' he said, giving Billy a stern look.

'Um, nose,' the lad finished.

'Hello Mr Charles. Millie and I were hoping to ride Stumps over to Chesterfield Downs this morning so we can train Bony and Chops,' Alice-Miranda explained.

'Mmm,' Charlie nodded. 'Why doesn't Billy here drive you? I'm afraid I don't have time and you'll never get Stumps back in this early. Mrs Parker's coming over to inspect the plant stocks for the show in a little while and I've still got a bit to do. Then we have a committee meeting over at her place.'

'Yes, Mrs Howard said you were busy,' Alice-Miranda said.

'The keys for the utility are hanging on the hook just inside the greenhouse.' Charlie motioned for the lad to go and get them.

'But I don't know where Chesterfield Downs is,' Billy protested.

'We do,' said Millie.

'But I haven't driven the ute before,' he said.

'You can drive, can't you, Billy?' Charlie asked.

'Yeah, of course,' Billy replied.

'Well then, get the keys and meet the girls at the front of the school,' Charlie said, exasperated. 'Or have you got somewhere else to be today?'

'No, I . . . no.' Billy shook his head. 'I'm happy to take them to Chesterfield Downs. The girls tell me it's pretty special.'

'Good, at least then I'll know where you are,' said Charlie. He'd begun to think the lad was a phantom, the number of times he seemed to just vanish.

Ten minutes later, Alice-Miranda and Millie were waiting on the steps at Winchesterfield Manor. The utility clattered down the driveway and rolled to a halt in front of them.

Both girls hopped into the front, with Millie in the middle.

'When we get to the end of the driveway you need to turn left,' said Alice-Miranda.

The car took off and then slowed to a stop at the gate before Billy turned left as instructed. He planted his foot on the accelerator and the vehicle sped up.

'Ooh, be careful, Billy,' said Millie anxiously. 'You might get a speeding ticket. Constable Derby likes to patrol this stretch of road.'

'I don't think he'll be there today,' Alice-Miranda remarked. 'Constable Derby and Mrs Derby have gone away for the weekend. It's Mrs Derby's sister's wedding in the city so they won't be back until tonight.'

'Is he the only copper in the village?' Billy asked.

'Yes,' Alice-Miranda replied, 'and he's quite the loveliest man you'll ever meet.'

Billy scoffed. 'I doubt it.'

'It's true, he really is. I know I'll feel better when he's back, what with all those carnival people around,' Millie said.

Billy glanced at the girl. 'What carnival people?'

She looked ahead pointedly, willing him to keep his eyes on the road. 'Yesterday when Alice-Miranda and I went riding we saw them. They've taken over the whole of Gertrude's Grove. One of the boys pushed Alice-Miranda over – that's how she got the bump on her head,' Millie explained.

'What boy?' Billy asked.

'His name's Pete and he got into a fight with another kid called Tarquin and a girl called Fern,' said Millie. 'Alice-Miranda got in the way and Fern did too.'

'Is she all right? The other girl?' Billy asked.

Alice-Miranda was surprised by his concern. 'I'm not sure. Her wrist could have been broken but she wouldn't let us help her. Do you know her?'

'No, of course not. Why would I? I just don't like hearing about people getting hurt,' Billy said brusquely.

'Some big guy called Alf came out and the kids all scattered like confetti,' Millie said. 'Anyway, I'll be glad when they move on.'

Alice-Miranda frowned at Millie. 'I'm sure they're perfectly lovely people.'

'Carnival people? That's not what I've heard,' Billy said. 'That Alf guy sounds a real thug and besides, everyone knows that if anything goes bad when the carnies are in town, you know exactly where to look.'

'I don't think that's fair at all,' Alice-Miranda disagreed.

'So where is this Gertrude's Grove place?' Billy asked.

'It's through the woods, over near Caledonia Manor,' Alice-Miranda replied.

All this talk of the carnival seemed to encourage Billy to drive even faster.

'That's the turn-off just up there,' said Millie. She was gripping the dashboard now.

He turned the car into the lane, barely reducing his speed at all.

'Mr Boots, perhaps you should slow down,' Alice-Miranda suggested. 'Otherwise you'll scare the horses.'

'There's the driveway!' Millie shouted, pointing at the gateposts on the right-hand side of the road.

Without any warning, Billy planted his foot on the brake. The car skidded to a halt and a veil of dust overtook them, enveloping the vehicle. Thankfully the girls were strapped in or they might have ended up through the windscreen.

There was a deathly silence.

'Sorry,' the young man said at last. 'I don't know what happened then. I just got distracted.'

Distracted by what, Alice-Miranda wondered. Perhaps Millie was right about Billy Boots? She had a strange feeling that there was more to him than she had first thought.

Billy drove through the main entrance and up the driveway at a snail's pace.

'Wow, this place is beautiful,' he said, his eyes scanning from one side of the road to the other.

'Wait until you see the house,' Millie said. She

sighed deeply, still catching her breath after Billy's wild driving. 'It's gorgeous but Aunty Gee hardly ever comes down here at all. Most of the time it's empty.'

As the car rounded the bend the house came into view.

'Whoa!' Billy exclaimed. 'It's a mansion and a half, in't it.'

Billy continued up the driveway and around to the parking area beside the stables.

'Geez, they make the stables at your place look like a chook shed,' Billy commented. 'Imagine being this rich!'

Alice-Miranda and Millie hopped out of the car.

'Would you like to come and meet Rockstar?' Alice-Miranda asked.

'Yeah, of course. It's not every day you get to see the world's greatest racehorse up close.'

'I'll just see if I can find someone,' Alice-Miranda said, and headed off in the direction of the stable doors. Millie followed her.

'This place is amazing, all right,' Billy said to himself.

Alice-Miranda peered into the half-light of the stable block. 'Hello,' she called. 'Is anyone here?'

Wally Whitstable backed out of one of the stalls close to the entrance, pulling a wheelbarrow full of soiled straw. 'Good morning, miss.'

'Did Bonaparte behave himself last night?' the tiny child asked.

'He's been quite the well-mannered guest,' Wally replied. 'Hello Millie. Your old Chops has been a good fellow too.'

Millie smiled and walked across to Chops's stall and hauled herself up onto the door. He was dozing with his head resting in the feed bin.

'It doesn't look like being here with all of these champions has rubbed off on him at all,' she said with a grin, before hopping down.

'Bonaparte must be just what the doctor ordered,' said Wally. 'I rode Rockstar again this morning. Freddy walked Bony down to the track and Rockstar ran like the wind.'

'That's wonderful,' Alice-Miranda grinned.

'So how did you get here?' Wally asked.

'Mr Boots drove us over. He's in the car,' Alice-Miranda informed him. 'Can he meet Rockstar?'

'I suppose so, but don't go into the stall,' Wally replied.

Alice-Miranda and Millie walked back outside

towards Billy, who was standing beside the driver's door.

Alice-Miranda beckoned to him. 'Mr Walt said you can come in.'

The trio entered the stable.

'Hello,' Wally nodded at the young man. 'How are you getting on over there at the school?'

'All right,' Billy Boots replied.

With track work long over for the day, most of the horses were now resting in their stalls.

'So who's who?' Billy asked as they walked the length of the block.

'That's Zelda and Boris and Fox,' Wally began.

'Geez, I've never heard of any of them,' Billy frowned. 'What is it, a herd of donkeys in here?'

'No, those are just their stable names. She's Royal Contessa at the track, that's Lord Beauregard and he's Foxleigh's Fancy,' said Wally, pointing them out one by one.

'Oh.' Billy nodded slowly as he recognised the champions. 'So why is Rockstar just Rockstar, then?'

'Apparently Queen Georgiana named him her-self and she thought it was perfect. That's why he doesn't have another name,' Wally explained. 'It's a bit unusual for a racehorse to have just one name.'

'I think it's perfect, too – he is a rock star,' Alice-Miranda agreed.

Dick Wigglesworth emerged from the tack room where an electrician was busy rewiring the switches. 'Hello there, who's this?'

'Hello Mr Wigglesworth,' Alice-Miranda greeted the silver-haired man with the bushy eyebrows. 'This is Mr Boots.'

Dick Wigglesworth stepped forward and shook hands firmly with Billy. 'Good to meet you,' Dick said with a nod. Billy returned the gesture but stayed silent.

'Mr Boots has just taken over from Mr Walt at school,' said Alice-Miranda.

'So you've come to meet our boy, have you?' Mr Wigglesworth walked over to the stall and opened the door.

'He ran his best split since the derby this morning,' Freddy piped up as he emerged from a stall that he'd been mucking out.

'That's wonderful,' said Alice-Miranda.

'I just held Bony at the side of the track. When Wally took off it was all he could do to hold him –

he just wanted to get back to his little mate here,' Freddy explained.

'Don't you have work to do, lad?' Dick frowned at the young man.

'Yes, sir,' he said and disappeared back inside to his pile of manure.

'Mr Wigglesworth, do you think it would be sensible to keep Bony here for a few more days?' Alice-Miranda asked. 'If it means that Rockstar has a chance at the Queen's Cup, I'd be happy for him to stay.'

'But the show starts in less than two weeks,' Millie complained. 'And we have to do some proper training for the pairs events or we'll be hopeless. I mean, Chops is no hacking champion at the best of times and we have to make sure they can actually stay in time with each other.'

'I'm sure we can work something out,' said Alice-Miranda.

'No, Alice-Miranda, I think you should take Bonaparte home with you today,' Dick Wigglesworth insisted.

Rockstar whinnied as if to protest.

'Are you sure, sir?' Wally asked. 'He seems much better with the company and when I told Miss Pepper what had happened on the telephone this morning she was thrilled.'

'When did you speak to Evelyn?' Mr Wigglesworth said crossly.

'She phoned when you were in the top paddock. She asked me what had been happening and so I told her all about Bony and Rockstar and she thought it was wonderful. She asked if Alice-Miranda would mind us keeping Bony for the week at least.'

'Did she now?' the foreman said. Rockstar leaned over the stall door and nibbled a sugar cube from his hand.

'So he's pretty quiet then?' Billy Boots enquired.

'No, he's a nutcase,' Freddy chimed in again as he emerged with a wheelbarrow full of soiled straw.

Dick Wigglesworth glared at Freddy, who gulped and disappeared back to his work.

Billy walked towards the stall and reached up to give the horse's ear a scratch. The giant leaned forward, throwing his head towards Billy and rubbing his neck against the top of the stall door.

'I don't believe it.' Dick looked at the giant beast and the young man. 'If I tried that he'd just as soon have my hand off.'

Rockstar sniffed Billy's hands and then his head.

'Look out!' Wally warned. 'You're likely to lose an ear if you're not careful.'

But the horse didn't bite Billy at all. He nibbled the lad's earlobe.

Dick shook his head. 'Well, that's the strangest thing. I've only ever seen Rockstar like that with Evelyn.'

'You must have a way with horses, Mr Boots,' said Alice-Miranda. 'Usually my Bonaparte can't stand young men either – no offence, it's just the way he is. And when he first met you I was afraid he was about to take a chunk out of your arm but he just gave you a lick instead. It was very odd indeed.'

Dick Wigglesworth frowned.

Billy shrugged and patted the champion's neck. 'You're a good boy, aren't you?' he whispered. 'Well, I'd best be off then. Thanks for the tour. Nice to meet you all.' Billy turned and headed towards the door. Alice-Miranda and Millie followed him outside to say goodbye and thank him for the lift.

The two girls watched as the ute drove down the driveway. Millie turned to Alice-Miranda. 'I'm glad we're not going back with him. He drives like a maniac.'

Alice-Miranda frowned. He was certainly an

interesting young man. 'Well, Bony and Rockstar seem to like him a lot, and you know neither of them like anyone much.'

Millie shook her head. 'I still say he's weird.'

'Come on, let's go and ask Mr Wigglesworth if there's somewhere around here we can ride,' suggested Alice-Miranda. 'Afterwards I'll leave Bonaparte and we can double back on Chops.'

Millie nodded and the girls walked back inside the cool building.

Chapter 16

Over at Myrtle Parker's house, the show committee meeting was about to commence. With the front sitting room sparkling and Newton the gnome in his special spot on top of the china cabinet, Myrtle was bustling about in the kitchen getting the tea tray ready. The only thing missing was her badge – she wished she could remember where she'd put it. It was most unlike her to lose things.

Mrs Howard, Doreen Smith and Charlie Weatherly had driven into the village together and were to be joined by Deidre Winterbottom, whose husband Wallace was the Headmaster at Fayle School for Boys, and Herman Munz, the owner of the general store. It was strange how each year the committee seemed to shrink in the exact same proportion that Myrtle's role expanded.

As Mrs Smith turned the Mini into Myrtle's driveway, Mrs Howard noticed a gangly, dark-haired girl standing on the other side of the street.

'I wonder who that is,' she said.

Charlie turned and stared out of the rear window. He was jammed into the back of the tiny car like a sardine in a tin. 'I don't recognise the lass.'

Mrs Smith looked into the rear-vision mirror and saw the child. 'She's probably one of the carnival children. She might be the same girl Alice-Miranda and Millie met yesterday. The girls spotted her again as we were driving out of Chesterfield Downs.'

'I heard that our little one had a run-in with one of the boys over there,' said Mrs Howard. 'Alice-Miranda didn't say a thing but Millicent couldn't wait to regale me with all the details.'

'You've got to feel sorry for the poor kids,' Charlie began.

'Sorry for them?' Doreen Smith scoffed. 'Why?'

'How would you like to spend your whole child-hood never having a proper place to call home? It must be hard to make friends. And then there's everyone always suspecting you of being up to no good and getting the blame for anything that goes wrong.'

Howie and Mrs Smith exchanged nods. They could see what Charlie meant.

'And I think it would be best if we kept this to ourselves. You know what Myrtle's like once she finds out that the carnival people are here,' Charlie warned them. 'I wonder where they've set up camp this time.'

'Gertrude's Grove, according to Millie,' Mrs Howard offered. 'I imagine they'll move to the showground by the weekend so that they can set everything up in time.'

The ladies agreed with Charlie about keeping the information quiet. There was no point giving Myrtle any more to fuss about.

Deidre Winterbottom drove into the driveway just as the group in front were getting out of the car.

'Good morning all,' Deidre called.

'Morning Deidre,' the others chorused.

'How's Wallace?' Charlie asked.

'Well, thank you, Charlie. He's off with the boys on a cadet camp this weekend so it's rather quiet at home with just Parsley for company.'

Parsley was Wallace's treasured West Highland terrier. 'I hate leaving him at home but I know Myrtle's not at all partial to dogs and I'd hate to upset her.'

The group crowded onto the front porch and Doreen rang the bell.

'I hope Herman's not going to be late again,' said Howie. 'I've got things to do back at school.'

'Coming,' Myrtle's shrill voice called from inside. She pulled open the door and a strong gust of perfume sent the visitors reeling.

'My goodness, Myrtle, what's that scent you're wearing?' Charlie asked.

'Do you like it? It's called Flower Show and it used to be Reginald's favourite when we were newly-weds. I thought it might help stir some memories,' Myrtle explained.

Herman Munz scooted up the front steps to join the group.

'Or more likely finish him off once and for all,' Charlie whispered in Herman's ear as the ladies followed Myrtle inside.

'Come through. Say hello to the visitors, Reginald,' she instructed her slumbering husband as they shuffled through the sitting room to the dining room.

Myrtle invited them all to sit down and began to pass out sheets of paper, which looked suspiciously like lists of jobs.

'Now, we have a lot to get through this morning,' she announced, then headed into the kitchen and returned with the teapot and a plate of plain biscuits. The teacups and saucers were already laid out around the table.

'I'm sorry, Myrtle, I should have brought something with me for our morning tea,' Mrs Smith apologised.

Myrtle pursed her lips. 'That *would* have been nice. Especially as I've been so busy taking Henrietta Fayle to her appointments here and there and then spending as much time as I can with Evelyn Pepper at the hospital.'

'How is she?' Deidre Winterbottom enquired.

'I think she's going to have a breakdown,' Myrtle informed the group. 'She's so worried about that silly old horse of hers.'

Mrs Smith couldn't help but interject. 'No, she's not.'

'She most certainly is,' Myrtle tutted. 'Ridiculously so.'

Doreen nodded. 'Yes, I'm sure she's concerned about Rockstar but she's nowhere near a breakdown.'

'And what gives you that impression, Doreen?' Myrtle looked up from where she was pouring the tea and glared at the cook.

'I saw her just yesterday and she's doing wonderfully well,' Mrs Smith replied.

Myrtle snorted. 'Doreen, why don't you take over pouring the tea and then we can get started. You're so much better at serving people.' Myrtle Parker smiled thinly and handed the teapot to Mrs Smith. 'Now, item one on the agenda: toilet facilities. Who's going to volunteer to clean them?'

Chapter 17

At Chesterfield Downs, Bonaparte had clearly demonstrated his unhappiness about leaving Rockstar. When Wally led him out of the stall the young man received a nasty nip on the arm for his trouble. The pony's vocal objections had been met with soft nickers from Rockstar, almost as though the big fellow knew that Alice-Miranda just wanted to take his friend out for a little while and then he'd be back. In fact, she'd whispered as much in Rockstar's ear.

And while Bony proved most difficult inside

the stable block, once Wally managed to get him outside the sunshine seemed to improve his mood. Alice-Miranda and Millie spent a couple of hours in the arena putting the ponies through their paces before Chops simply stopped in his tracks and refused to budge. The girls had practised their pairs work over and over and had the two ponies walking, trotting and cantering in tandem better than they had ever done before. But when Chops had had enough, no amount of encouragement – kicks, treats or otherwise – could make him move.

'Come on, Millie, he's worked hard this morning and I'm sure that Rockstar will be missing this fellow, too,' Alice-Miranda called.

When Bony and Alice-Miranda began to move towards the stables, Chops suddenly got the urge to move and even managed a trot to catch up with his friend.

Their arrival was met by a piercing whinny from Rockstar. Bony replied and while Alice-Miranda gave him a quick rub down, the two black beauties had a lovely conversation in whinnies and nickers and neighs. Millie let Chops have a rest in the stall where he had spent the night and the girls headed off to find Wally and say goodbye.

They looked in the feed room and the tack room, but there was no sign of him. All of the lads had disappeared, no doubt for lunch. At the end of the stable block Alice-Miranda could see a light on in the mezzanine level upstairs.

She wondered if Mr Wigglesworth might be in his office.

As the two girls started to climb the staircase, there was a loud howl. 'Arooooooooooo!' Keith went on for an age.

'What are you doing up here, old fellow?' Alice-Miranda asked as she gave him a pat. At the top of the stairs was a small landing and two offices. Both doors were closed but nameplates indicated who they belonged to.

'He's got such sad eyes,' Millie remarked as she kneeled beside Keith and gave him a scratch under his chin.

'He's a basset hound – they *always* look sad,' Alice-Miranda replied. 'But I think perhaps Keith really is at the moment. He must be missing Miss Pepper.' Alice-Miranda had already noted that the hound was sitting outside the door which bore the name plate *Evelyn Pepper, Trainer-Manager*.

Alice-Miranda knocked at the other door, which had a brass plate saying *Dick Wigglesworth, Stable Foreman.*

'Hello,' a voice called from within.

Alice-Miranda poked her head around the door. 'Hello Mr Wigglesworth, it's just us.' She opened the door further. 'We've come to say goodbye but we couldn't find Wally or any of the lads and we just wanted to tell someone that we were heading off.'

Dick swivelled around in his chair and beckoned for the girls to enter.

Keith began to howl again.

'For heaven's sake, Keith! Keep that noise down, you silly old so-and-so. We *all* miss her,' he yelled at the mutt, who stopped his howling.

The girls entered the office. There was a huge window looking down onto the stables. Mr Wigglesworth sat at an enormous walnut desk and there were a couple of green leather tub chairs opposite him. The walls on three sides were lined with photographs. All featured horses, most of which had a woman standing beside them.

'Is that Miss Pepper?' Alice-Miranda pointed at a photograph of a very handsome bay horse and a gorgeous young woman with cascading blonde curls and a stylish trilby hat.

'Yes, that's Ev with her first Group One winner at the Dunhill Guineas. A bay mare called Royal Flush.'

'She's beautiful,' Alice-Miranda remarked.

'She always has been,' Dick muttered under his breath.

'Sorry, Mr Wigglesworth, what did you say?' Alice-Miranda asked.

'Beautiful horse that Royal Flush,' he said.

'Miss Pepper looks rather lovely too,' Alice-Miranda added.

'Oh yes, I dare say she does,' Dick replied. 'But I hadn't noticed.'

Alice-Miranda walked around the room looking at the pictures and reading the engraved brass plates beneath them. She found Mr Wigglesworth's last comment a little hard to believe, given how many of the photographs were *of* Miss Pepper.

'Are you married, Mr Wigglesworth?' Alice-Miranda asked.

'No. Suppose I just never found a woman who could put up with the crazy hours of a stable foreman.'

'How long have you worked for Aunty Gee?' asked Alice-Miranda.

'Feels like forever. I think I started the year after Ev came to work here,' he replied.

'You must be a pretty amazing team,' said Alice-Miranda, watching Mr Wigglesworth seriously. He immediately looked away.

'I suppose we are.' He fingered a brochure that was sitting on his desk. Alice-Miranda couldn't see what it was, but he was staring at it intently.

'So do you think Rockstar really has a chance next Sunday?' Millie asked as she plonked herself down in one of the tub chairs opposite Mr Wigglesworth.

'Gosh, where did you two come from? Scotland Yard?'

Millie and Alice-Miranda giggled.

'He's never been to the track without Evelyn,' Dick said finally.

'Is it true that the Queen's Cup is the only trophy Her Majesty doesn't have?' Millie asked.

'Yes,' Dick nodded. 'And I think she might have to wait another year yet. Have we finished? Don't you two have to get going?'

'There's no hurry, Mr Wigglesworth,' Alice-

Miranda said as she sat down beside Millie. 'And I think Rockstar will win for sure. And Miss Pepper might be out of hospital by race day anyway.'

Dick frowned. 'I think you're wrong there, young lady, on two counts. It's very unlikely that horse will win and Evelyn needs to stay put until the doctors give her the all-clear. I don't want her back here until she's fully recovered. I know what she's like. She'll push herself too hard, like she always does.'

Alice-Miranda considered what she'd observed of Mr Wigglesworth. She wondered if Miss Pepper felt the same way about him as he obviously did about her.

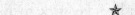

The girls gave Keith a farewell pat and headed down-stairs. Alice-Miranda checked on Bony and Rockstar, who were standing in their side-by-side stalls, heads over the door looking at each other. Chops was dozing but Millie had the old boy saddled in no time and managed to entice him out into the open air with the aid of a couple of sugar cubes. She hopped onto his back and held out her hand for Alice-Miranda to climb up behind her.

Together they walked down the long driveway and turned left into the shady lane. Chops's rest had obviously done him good, as he marched along at a fair pace. Alice-Miranda thought it would be fun to try to get him to canter but Millie was worried that her tiny friend might slide straight off his bare backside.

The girls chatted about how they might get in enough practice for the show and when they would have time to get over and ride together again.

'You'll have to remind me to ask Mrs Derby if she can help us with all the entry forms for the show tomorrow morning,' Millie said. 'I've heard that Mrs Parker's really finicky about them.'

'I suppose she just likes to stick to the rules,' Alice-Miranda said as she watched the passing countryside. 'When did Mrs Parker's husband die?'

'He's not dead,' Millie replied.

'What do you mean? Yesterday at Caledonia Manor she said something about her husband having been at the same hospital as Miss Pepper and then she said "God rest his weary soul".' Alice-Miranda tried to lean forward to look at Millie.

'That's weird. It's a long story but her husband's in a coma and she keeps him in the sitting room,'

Millie stated, as though it was the most usual thing in the world.

Alice-Miranda's mind was in a whirl. 'Poor Mrs Parker, that's a terrible predicament.'

'Poor Mr Parker, I say. Imagine having that woman talking at you all day every day. It's no wonder he'd rather be asleep.'

'There must be a medical reason for it,' Alice-Miranda reasoned. 'You can't just will yourself to be in a coma – well, I don't think you can.'

'Mrs Howard says that the doctors can't work it out and there's no reason in the world why he shouldn't wake up. It is strange, isn't it?' said Millie.

As Chops neared the school gate, Alice-Miranda noticed a girl walking along the side of the road ahead of them. 'Is that Fern?' she asked.

'If it is she can keep walking,' Millie muttered.

'I'd like to talk to her,' Alice-Miranda said. 'I wonder if her arm's all right.'

'She doesn't want to talk to you, Alice-Miranda. She made that perfectly clear yesterday.'

'I just want to say hello.' Alice-Miranda slipped off Chops's rump and began jogging. 'Fern,' she called.

On hearing her name the raven-haired girl

turned and then, realising who it was, kept walking.

Alice-Miranda was only a few metres away from her now.

'I just want to talk to you for a minute,' Alice-Miranda called again.

Fern spun around as Alice-Miranda caught up to her. 'What do you want?' she glowered.

'Hello,' said Alice-Miranda. 'I know you were upset yesterday but I just wanted to see if you were okay.' She glanced at Fern's bandaged wrist.

'Why wouldn't I be?' The girl narrowed her amber eyes, like a cat eyeing its prey.

'I'm sorry about what happened. I didn't mean to cause a fuss,' Alice-Miranda apologised.

Fern didn't know what to say. People didn't apologise to her. They usually asked her and Tarquin to move along, get off their property and leave their kids alone. She fiddled with a stray strand of hair and held her sore wrist to her chest.

'Has anyone taken a look at that?' Alice-Miranda asked.

The gangly girl lowered her eyes and shook her head.

'Did you bandage it yourself?'
She nodded.

'Goodness, you must be an expert at bandages. If I had to do it on myself I'm sure I'd end up looking like a mummy with a ham on the end of its arm,' Alice-Miranda said with a smile.

A picture of an Ancient Egyptian mummy invaded Fern's mind, with its hands bandaged like two giant hams. She tried to smother a smile.

'Would you like to come up to the school so I can ask Mrs Howard to take a look at it?' Alice-Miranda offered. 'She used to be a nurse.'

Fern shook her head. Her wrist was throbbing and the bruise had deepened and was now a kaleidoscope of purple and yellow along with the black. But medical stuff cost money and she didn't have any – and she wasn't about to ask Alf for any either.

As if reading her mind, Alice-Miranda made her a tempting offer: 'It won't cost anything – and if you have to go to the doctor, I'm sure that we can work something out.'

'Why do you even care?' Fern said suspiciously.

'Because you're hurt and I'd do the same thing for anyone,' Alice-Miranda replied.

'I don't need you to feel sorry for me just because I live with the carnival,' Fern frowned.

'Gosh, I hope you don't think that. I'm rather

jealous of you, actually. I think it would be wonderful to travel all over the place and meet loads of people and I'm sure you must be able to go on lots of rides too. I mean, the carnival always makes children happy,' Alice-Miranda babbled.

'Is that what you really think?' Fern whispered.

'What do you mean?'

'Most people hate it when we come to town and we always get blamed for things that go wrong and stuff,' Fern explained.

'Well, I think that's very unfair,' Alice-Miranda said. 'If people just took the time to get to know you, then every year when you come back to the village they could catch up with you as friends.'

Millie had been watching Alice-Miranda and the dark-haired girl from a distance. They seemed to be having quite a long conversation. She slipped down off Chops and walked towards them, leading the pony behind her.

'So where's your horse?' Fern asked Alice-Miranda.

'I've left him over at Chesterfield Downs. He's keeping Rockstar company for a little while. For some reason they've taken quite a shine to one another and he's helping get Rockstar out of his dark mood,' Alice-Miranda explained.

'Who's Rockstar?' Fern asked.

'He's a beautiful stallion, and a rather exciting racehorse,' Alice-Miranda replied.

Fern's ears pricked up. '*Oh*. I *have* heard of him. Isn't he supposed to be the best racehorse in the world?' Fern offered just a small titbit about her life: 'Alf always bets on him. And he always wins, too.'

Alice-Miranda heard the clip-clop of hooves as Chops approached. 'Millie, you remember Fern from yesterday.'

'Yeah,' Millie said curtly.

'I said that Fern should come up to the house with us and let Mrs Howard take a look at her wrist,' Alice-Miranda explained.

Fern eyed Millie nervously. The red-haired girl didn't seem nearly as friendly as the little one with the chocolate curls. Fern shook her head. 'No.'

She began to walk away.

'You should come,' Millie said.

Fern stopped and looked over her shoulder.

'I don't bite, you know,' Millie said. 'Chops might, but I promise I haven't bitten anyone since I was a toddler.'

Fern tried hard not to smile.

'Come on.' Alice-Miranda reached out to hold Fern's good hand.

The girl looked at her and pulled a face. 'What are you doing?'

'Well, now that we're friends I thought you might let me hold your hand. It's what friends do.'

Fern's amber eyes filled with tears. She tried hard to blink them back but one fell with a plop onto her cheek.

'I'm sorry, did I hurt you?' Alice-Miranda asked.

Fern brushed the moisture away. 'No.'

'Come on, then, let's go and find Mrs Howard and see about that wrist.'

Chapter 18

Alice-Miranda suggested that Millie ride Chops back to the stables and meet her and Fern at the house.

As they walked up the driveway, Alice-Miranda pointed out various landmarks around the school. 'That's the library over there with the clock tower. It's almost new but it looks like it's been here for as long as the rest of the buildings, and that's Winchesterfield Manor where Miss Grimm has her study and the flat attached where she lives with her husband, Mr Grump.'

'Are you serious?' Fern asked. 'Your headmistress is called Miss Grimm and her husband is Mr Grump? They sound like a match made in heaven. Not!'

'Oh, they are,' Alice-Miranda nodded. 'They have the most romantic love story ever. I'll tell you about it one day. And that's the dining room at the back of the courtyard and some of the classrooms and over there, that's Grimthorpe House where we all live.'

Fern's eyes widened as she took it all in. 'Do you like it here?' she asked her guide.

'Oh yes, it's the most wonderful school in the world, except for Mrs Kimmel's in New York – it's amazing too. I've just spent a month there,' Alice-Miranda chattered.

'In America, you mean?' Fern asked.

'Yes. Mummy and Daddy were there for business and so I got to go for a month too and see what school's like there and explore the city.'

Fern could hardly imagine such a thing. 'Are your parents rich?' she asked.

Alice-Miranda thought for a moment. 'I suppose if you mean are they rich because they have a lot of money, then yes, my parents both run big businesses and they employ lots of people. But I think everyone's rich in their own way,' she replied. 'We all have things that we're good at and ways we can help people. You don't have to have lots of money to be rich.'

Fern pondered the child's response. She and Tarquin weren't rich. Sometimes she thought it would be nice to try it for a while. But she was glad that they had each other.

Alice-Miranda led the way to Grimthorpe House. Along the front veranda a long rack played host to several pairs of joggers and some riding boots. An old church pew stood on the other side of the large black front door. There was a buzzer beside it and a giant lion's head knocker in the middle. But Alice-Miranda did not buzz or knock; she simply turned the handle and opened the front door. The child wiped her feet on the doormat and walked into the hallway. Fern stood outside on the path.

'Come on.' Alice-Miranda smiled and nodded towards the door. 'I'll just go and find Mrs Howard. You can wait in my room if you like.'

Fern hesitated, as if her feet were stuck in wet cement.

'It's all right, really it is,' Alice-Miranda promised.

The taller girl took a few steps towards the veranda and then scurried across the threshold and into the hallway, as if by merely entering the building something terrible might happen to her.

Alice-Miranda led the way down to her and Millie's room.

Fern was surprised by how plain it was. White walls, bare timber floors with a small rug and practical furniture. She had been expecting something much fancier – like the time her mother took her to have a peek inside a historic mansion that was having an open day. She had spent the entire time with her mouth open, hardly believing that anyone actually lived in a place as fancy as that.

'You can sit on the bed or the chair over there,' Alice-Miranda instructed. 'I'll be back in a minute.'

Alice-Miranda scampered out the door and headed to the sitting room at the rear of the house but Mrs Howard wasn't there. She ducked into the downstairs kitchenette but it was empty too. Alice-Miranda ran upstairs to Mrs Howard's flat, where she knocked at the door but it seemed that she wasn't at home. In fact, Alice-Miranda hadn't encountered a single girl either. But it wasn't unusual for the house to be deserted on a Sunday afternoon with girls off doing this and that.

Downstairs, Fern was looking around the room. She picked up the photographs beside Alice-Miranda's bed, which she assumed were of the child's mother and father. She felt her chest tighten as she thought about her own mother.

Fern had loved her more than anything in the world. But now she was gone. She wandered over to look at the ornaments on top of the dressing table. There were some tiny figurines of cats in different positions. She picked one up and held it in her hand. It was a grey tabby with a smug look on its face. She'd feel smug if she lived here too, Fern thought.

Out the front of the house, the garden gate clanged as Mrs Howard charged up the path, pushed open the door and blustered into the building.

'Myrtle Parker will be the death of me – this list of jobs is as long as my left arm.' The words bubbled and frothed on Howie's lips. 'I need a cup of tea, and not that awful dishwater Myrtle serves up – a proper strong brew.' She barged her way along the hall. 'And when will I get all of my work done here, now that she's taken up most of the day with her petty little meeting and all those ridiculous questions?' Upon seeing the door to Alice-Miranda and Millie's room open, Howie stopped.

'Alice-Miranda, Millicent, are you back?' She walked into the room to find a dark-haired girl standing next to Alice-Miranda's dressing table.

Fern heard the voice and froze.

'Hello, may I help you?' Mrs Howard looked the child up and down. She was tall and lean with the darkest of hair and the most unusual tawny-coloured eyes. 'Are you looking for something?'

Fern shook her head.

'May I ask what you're doing here?' The house-mistress had started to wonder about the child. She was very poorly dressed and seemed to be clutch-ing something in her hand. 'What's that you're holding?'

Fern knew what was coming next. She was about to be accused of something she hadn't done.

She threw the cat onto the bed and made a run for the door.

'Where do you think you're going?' cried Howie as the girl ducked under her outstretched arms and fled along the hallway. 'Come back here, young lady!'

On hearing Howie's shouts, Alice-Miranda raced

downstairs to find Mrs Howard standing at the open front door.

'What's the matter, Mrs Howard? Where's Fern?' Alice-Miranda asked.

'Fern?' the housemistress repeated.

'Yes, my friend Fern. I brought her back to the house with me because I thought you could have a look at her arm. I think it might be badly injured and it was my fault because I asked the boy to play football and then she got into an argument with Pete.' Alice-Miranda finally paused to take a breath.

'Oh dear,' Howie replied. 'I'm afraid that she's run off. She was in your room holding one of your little cat ornaments and I asked her what was in her hand.'

Alice-Miranda and Mrs Howard looked at one another, knowing full well the implication of Mrs Howard's question to Fern.

'I have to find her and tell her it was all a misunderstanding,' said Alice-Miranda hurriedly. She ran down the path towards the gate. 'Fern!' she called. 'Fern, please stop, Mrs Howard didn't mean anything.'

The child dashed onto the driveway and saw the older girl in the distance. She had almost reached

gates. Alice-Miranda ran as quickly as she
could, calling out all the way, but Fern seemed deter-
mined to ignore her.

'Fern, please stop,' Alice-Miranda cried. 'You
didn't do anything wrong. It was just a misunderstanding. Mrs Howard didn't mean anything.'

By the time Alice-Miranda reached the road,
the tall girl had completely disappeared from view.
Alice-Miranda looked towards the village and in the
other direction towards the railway line but it was as
if Fern had vanished.

Fern ran and ran until she finally allowed herself a
moment to catch her breath. Something told her
that she shouldn't have run away, but it was instinc-
tive. It wouldn't have mattered if she had tried to
explain. It never did. She looked up and realised
that she was in the middle of the village, standing
opposite the church with its pretty stone gate and
stained glass windows. A climbing rose grew along
the fence and the hedge was neatly trimmed. Beside
the church, the graveyard grew its own granite garden
of crosses and headstones.

Without thinking, she crossed the road pushed open the gate. It was as if her legs were tak her somewhere that she really didn't want to go, bu she had no power to stop them.

The graves at the front of the cemetery dated back over a century but towards the rear the newer inhabitants took their place. A small temporary cross bearing her name and the year of her birth and death was all that remained of Fern's mother Gina. Alf had said that he would arrange a proper headstone but Fern knew that he never would. That cross made of timber would eventually rot away and there would be nothing to mark the spot at all. Tendrils of grass had inched their way across the mound of compacted earth.

Fern knelt in front of the grave. Tears sprouted from her eyes and ran like rivers down her cheeks.

'Why did you go?' she sobbed. 'Why?'

Up until now Fern hadn't cried for her mother. She hadn't allowed it.

'Be strong for your brothers,' her mother had told her as she closed her eyes and fell asleep forever, and so Fern had been. But now in the stillness of the cemetery, her grief poured out of her like a waterfall.

...rled up into a ball and lay on the warm

...ern had no idea how long she had been there
...en a voice interrupted her dream-filled slumber.
It was a man. Fern opened her eyes and realised that
the light was fading. Her wrist was throbbing a dull
drumbeat.

'Fern,' the voice whispered.

Fern looked around. She wondered if she was
still dreaming.

'I'm over here,' the voice whispered again.

She sat up and could see the outline of a young
man heading towards her.

She rubbed her eyes. 'Liam? Is it really you?'

The lad rushed forward and wrapped his
arms around Fern, tears spilling down both their
cheeks.

'Where have you been?' she asked.

'It doesn't matter.' He looked at her bandaged
arm. 'Are you all right?'

'It's nothing. It's getting better, I'm sure.' She
stepped back and looked at him. 'You know you
can't be here. If Alf finds out I don't know what he'll
do.' Fern's heart was hammering inside her chest.

'I know. But don't worry. I'm going to make

things right and Alf's going to get what's coming to him.' The lad blinked back more tears. 'But I need you to help me. I need you to do whatever I ask you to – no questions.'

Fern gulped.

'You don't think I actually did what he said?' the young man asked, studying Fern's face closely.

She frowned. 'No, of course not.'

'I didn't do it, Fern. I didn't take all that money. You know me better than that.' He placed his arms on her shoulders. 'Will you help me?'

Fern nodded. She wanted to believe her brother more than anything. 'Where will you be?' she asked.

'It's best you don't know. But tell Tarq that I love him and I'll find you when I need to.' He hugged Fern again, then turned and disappeared among the headstones.

Fern felt as if she could hardly breathe. She hadn't realised just how much she missed him.

She scurried out of the churchyard towards the village, hoping that Alf was too busy to notice her absence.

Chapter 19

Alice-Miranda had arrived back at the house to find Mrs Howard and Millie in the downstairs kitchenette making tea.

'I couldn't find her,' the younger girl explained. 'I'd hate for her to think that she was going to be accused of something.'

Mrs Howard frowned. 'My dear, I didn't accuse the girl of anything. I simply asked her what was in her hand.'

But Alice-Miranda knew that question alone

would have been enough to make Fern run.

'Have you checked our room?' Millie asked. 'Maybe she had stolen something and the cat ornament was just a decoy.'

'I'm sure she wouldn't have taken anything,' Alice-Miranda replied. 'She was so nervous about coming up in the first place.'

'You don't really know anything about her, Alice-Miranda.' Millie sipped the milky tea that Mrs Howard had just placed in front of her. 'Except that she has a really weird brother and she lives with the carnival people.'

Alice-Miranda frowned. 'Can you imagine what it would be like to be accused of doing the wrong thing all the time? That must be terrible.'

Mrs Howard placed a second cup on the small dining table and sat down. 'If the child comes back, Alice-Miranda, then of course I'll look at her wrist,' Howie offered. 'But if not, I think you should leave things alone this time. The carnival folk keep to themselves and I'm afraid I have enough to worry about this week with the show coming up and Myrtle Parker bossing me about, without having to keep an extra-close eye on you and your adventures.'

'But I just want to let her know she's not in trouble,' Alice-Miranda began.

Howie was firm. 'I'm sorry, Alice-Miranda, but I want you to stay away from Gertrude's Grove and concentrate on getting Bonaparte ready for the show. You can't save everyone, my dear.' Howie looked up and locked eyes with Alice-Miranda. 'Now, why don't you run along and get ready for dinner and Millie and I will finish our tea. Although I can't imagine what poor Mrs Smith will be able to cobble together now.'

'Why do you say that?' Millie asked.

'Well, our committee meeting at Myrtle Parker's ran for over seven hours. Seven hours!' Howie's face was getting redder and redder by the second. 'Can you imagine what could take that long? Myrtle assigned jobs to everyone. I'm sure that if poor Reginald had even blinked he'd have been given something to do as well . . .'

Millie wished she hadn't asked. *Wait for me*, she mouthed to her friend.

Alice-Miranda nodded, then excused herself to go and get changed. Millie began to push her chair back.

'You're not going to leave yet, Millicent, you haven't finished your tea,' Howie blustered on. 'And then . . .'

Millie glanced at the clock on the wall. Howie was wound up like a spring and she was going to tell the whole story whether Millie wanted to hear it or not. The child was well and truly stuck.

As Fern neared the crest of the hill above the camp site, she could hear laughter and shouting. Her mind was reeling. She was trying to remember exactly what happened that afternoon almost a year ago. Alf had argued with her older brother and then in the morning he was gone and Alf said that he'd run away because he'd been up to no good. The rest of the camp had blamed him for the missing carnival takings too.

In the fading afternoon light a swarm of children chased after the football on the open field. Someone had built a giant fire, ringed by rocks, closer to the caravans.

Fern scanned the scene, looking for her younger brother. He wouldn't be near the fire – he was scared of the flames. She assumed he was probably off somewhere playing with his badges. Fern spotted Alf with a bottle in his hand, laughing and carrying on with Doug Kessler beside him on a surprisingly smart-looking garden bench. No doubt Mrs Kessler would be in their caravan getting dinner ready for the six mouths she had to feed. Doug Kessler was a nice enough bloke but not one for domestic duties. A lot like Alf, Fern thought to herself. She couldn't remember him ever offering to get a meal or wash any clothes. Her mother used to take care of all that and now it was up to Fern.

Fern was hoping to get home without being noticed, but Alf had ears like radar and she knew it wouldn't be easy.

As she crept towards the caravan door, she thought she'd got away with it.

'Fern, Fernie, be a love and get me and Dougie another drink,' the old man yelled.

Fern's shoulders slumped.

'And where's that good-for-nothing brother of yours?' Alf called after her as she entered the caravan. She marched across to the fridge, wondering herself where Tarquin could be. Fern collected two bottles of beer and walked back outside.

'You're a good girl, Fernie, aren't you, love?' said Alf with a toothy smile as he took the bottles and handed one to Doug. For a moment she saw a glimpse of the man her mother had fallen in love with. But it only lasted a moment.

'Have you seen Tarquin?' she asked.

'No, that's why I asked you where the moron was.' Alf twisted the cap off the beer bottle and took a swig. 'I thought he must have been with you.'

'No,' Fern winced. She clenched her fists into a ball. She hated when Alf called her brother names but there was no point saying anything. Alf would just do it more often.

Fern ran over to where the kids were finishing up their game.

'Has anyone seen Tarq?' she called.

A couple of older boys shook their heads and a cacophony of 'no's came back to her.

'I saw him,' Ivy said.

'Where?' Fern asked. 'How long ago?'

'What are you gonna give me?' Ivy challenged the older girl.

'Nothing, you little brat. Just tell me where you saw him.' Fern could feel her temperature rising. Ivy had that effect on her. In fact, she seemed to have that effect on most of the other children in the camp too.

Ivy's family, like Fern's, were from a long line

of travelling show people. The Joyces's carousel was renowned as one of the most beautiful in the country and had been in their family for over one hundred years. Ivy's father, Jim Joyce, always said that if it wasn't for him and his carousel no one would bother coming to the show. But everyone knew that wasn't true. The other rides might not have looked as lovely but they were a lot more popular with the younger patrons. Jim often got into spats with Alf about how things should be run and where the rides should be placed on the showgrounds. Six-year-old Ivy had inherited her father's bluster. No one wanted to play with her, but no one wanted to be on the receiving end of her parents' nastiness either. And so they all put up with her – most of the time.

But today Fern wasn't in the mood for an argument. 'Look, Ivy, just tell me where you saw him. I'll give you a chocolate.'

Fern was trying to remember if she had any lollies or chocolates stashed anywhere. It must have been the worst kept secret in the camp that if you wanted Ivy to do anything for you, you gave her something sweet.

'What sort?' Ivy asked, although Fern knew she wasn't fussy. Ivy's mother and father had her on a strict diet but little did they know that she was always scrounging junk from everyone else.

Fern remembered that she'd hidden some chocolate buttons in the cupboard beside her bed. She jogged over to the caravan and retrieved the little white bag.

'Here.' Fern handed the bag to Ivy. 'So where did you see him?'

'He walked over the top of the hill.' Ivy thrust her hand inside the bag and stuffed the chocolate treats one after the other into her mouth.

'You're lying.' Fern reached out and snatched the bag from Ivy's hand.

'Am not!' Ivy reached up and tried to grab the bag back again, but Fern held it high. 'He asked if he could play football and Pete told him to get lost.'

Fern gasped.

'Then he just disappeared.'

'How long ago?' Fern demanded.

Ivy screwed up her face. 'I don't know.'

Fern stamped her foot in frustration. 'Come on, Ivy, think. I'm sure you're not as stupid as you look.'

'I'm not stupid. You are!' Ivy retaliated.

'Ivy, I didn't mean it. Please just tell me when you saw him.' Fern was desperate.

'I went inside to have lunch and it was late

because Mum cooked a roast, then me and Mum were watching *Winners Are Grinners* and then Mum told me to go outside and play so it was just after that,' said Ivy.

'So it was a couple of hours ago?' Fern asked.

'I suppose so.' Ivy shrugged. 'He went that way,' she said, pointing to the top of the hill.

Fern's stomach twisted. The kids knew they couldn't say that to Tarquin. *Get lost.* He'd do it. She would have to tell Alf. It was getting dark and Tarquin could be anywhere.

Chapter 20

Hephzibah was pottering in the front garden, adding some bulbs to one of the freshly planted beds, when she looked up and spotted a dark-haired lad over by the fountain. He was sitting on the grass looking at something on the ground. She hauled herself to her feet and went to speak to him.

The old woman wasn't alone; several of her feline friends were lazing nearby. She'd lost count long ago of how many cats lived at Caledonia Manor, although with the teaching college about to open, she thought it might be time to find new homes for most of her furry companions.

Hephzibah was wearing light khaki trousers, a long-sleeved white shirt and a wide-brimmed hat to protect her face. Since meeting Alice-Miranda earlier in the year she no longer dressed from head to toe in black and had abandoned the veil that once covered her face.

'Hello there,' the old woman called as she walked across the lawn towards the boy. 'Can I help you?'

As she approached him, Hephzibah could see a cat rubbing against the lad's back. He didn't seem to have noticed it, so mesmerised was he by whatever was in front of him. Perhaps it was a tortoise, Hephzibah thought hopefully. It would be lovely to have some more wildlife in the garden.

The boy didn't seem to hear her and Hephzibah wondered if he might be deaf.

'Excuse me, are you all right?' she asked, as she drew closer.

The boy moved his head sideways and looked at her. He had the most extraordinary amber-coloured eyes. Just like a cat, she thought to herself.

Hephzibah could now see that he was looking at a collection of badges, neatly lined up in rows.

She tried again to get his attention. 'My name is Hephzibah and this is my home.' She wondered if this was the boy Alice-Miranda and Millie had told her about yesterday. 'Are you Tarquin?'

The boy looked up again. He didn't smile but there was a lightness about his eyes.

He nodded but then his face fell.

'What's the matter?' Hephzibah asked.

Tarquin stood up, then slowly pointed at her face. He reached up. Hephzibah stood perfectly still as the boy touched her scarred cheek.

'What's that?' he asked seriously.

'A scar.' Hephzibah smiled at him. 'It doesn't hurt.'

He looked back at her. Hephzibah wondered if something had happened to Tarquin, whether he had been born this way or, perhaps like her, there had been an accident. But her scars were only superficial; whatever was different about Tarquin affected him much more deeply.

'Do you like cats?' Hephzibah asked, watching as the tabby smooched up against the boy's leg.

He nodded and reached down to give the creature a rub on the top of its head. Then he launched into a monologue about cats, their history and what they eat and just about anything else you might care to know about the animals.

'My goodness,' Hephzibah interrupted him. 'You're very well informed about cats. Do you know about lots of creatures?'

Tarquin nodded.

'You must have walked a long way,' Hephzibah said, remembering that Millie and Alice-Miranda said that the camp was over at Gertrude's Grove.

The boy shrugged. 'I'm lost. Pete told me to get lost and so I am.'

Oh dear, Hephzibah thought. It would be best to take him up to the house and see if Mr Weatherly could come over from the school and drive him back to the Grove. It was a long way on foot and she certainly couldn't manage it herself.

'Would you like something to eat?' Hephzibah asked the boy. 'I have some cake.'

At the mention of the word, the boy's eyes lit up and he nodded.

'I like cake,' he said.

'Well then, dear, come with me.'

Hephzibah watched as he packed his badges away. One by one, he polished each of them with a handkerchief, then placed them into the plastic bag. She waited for him to finish, then led the way back to the house with the young lad and several cats following.

As always, more cats were asleep in various sunny spots along the path and the veranda. Tarquin stopped and patted each and every one of them.

'I hope you like chocolate cake,' said Hephzibah as they reached the kitchen door. He crossed the threshold and she motioned for him to sit at the kitchen table, which he studied intently.

Henrietta had gone to her room for a rest, so it was just the old woman and the young boy. Hephzibah lifted the large glass dome from the cake stand and cut a generous slice, which she slid onto a plate and placed in front of the lad.

'What do you think?' she said, hoping that he would look up.

Tarquin's eyes flickered but without so much as a glance her way he shovelled the chocolate confection into his mouth, hoovering up all the crumbs.

Hephzibah smiled at the performance. 'Goodness, you must be hungry.'

He didn't reply. Tarquin's tongue probed the edges of his mouth to make sure that he'd got every last morsel.

'Would you like some more?' she asked.

He nodded, and then, as if remembering that he'd forgotten something important, he said, 'Please.'

Hephzibah delivered another piece of cake and watched him consume it at a similar speed to the first. She then gave him a tall glass of milk. Surely that and the two slices of cake would see him full.

Tarquin gulped the chilled white liquid and finished with a loud 'ahhh'.

'Now, my dear boy, I'm going to call a friend and see if he can drive you back to your camp site,' Hephzibah explained. 'I don't think you should try to walk back. It will be dark soon and I'd hate for you to get lost in the woods overnight.'

The old woman walked over to the telephone and pressed 6. Alice-Miranda and Millie had set up speed dial for everyone at the school and all of the other numbers she might need.

'Hello Mr Weatherly, it's Hephzibah Fayle,' she spoke into the receiver. 'I have a favour to ask.'

Chapter 21

Alice-Miranda changed out of her dirty jodhpurs and shirt and into a clean pair of jeans and her favourite white 'I love New York' T-shirt. She checked the clock beside her bed and decided there was still time before dinner to see Mr Charles and ask if she might cut some flowers. She wanted to give them to Mrs Smith as a thank-you for all the lovely things she was doing to help her and Miss Pepper. She'd been hoping that Millie would be free to go and see Charlie with her but Mrs Howard had seemed especially keen for Millie's company.

Alice-Miranda walked down to the kitchenette and sitting room at the back of the house. Millie was gone and so was Mrs Howard, along with any evidence of their tea, but Ashima and Susannah had just arrived back from their afternoon's adventures.

'Hello,' Alice-Miranda greeted the girls. 'Have you seen Millie or Mrs Howard?'

'Yes, Howie had Millie and Jacinta and Sloane with her and they were heading to the laundry. My granny just dropped us back at school so it was lucky we had to take our bags to our room or we would have had to go too,' Ashima explained.

'Howie didn't look very happy,' Susannah added.

'No, she's had a busy day with the show committee and I think that's put her behind with her work,' said Alice-Miranda.

The laundry building was located at the rear of Grimthorpe House. It was rather like a cave, and had been a scullery and servants' quarters long before the house became part of the boarding school. Alice-Miranda was torn. She wanted to go and help her friends but she also wanted to see Mr Charles.

She decided to see him first and then head back to the laundry.

Alice-Miranda jogged across to the cobblestoned courtyard, past the dining room and through the stone archway that led to the greenhouse. It was getting late and she didn't know whether Mr Charles would still be there. But in the distance she could see someone moving pots about.

'Hello Mr Charles,' Alice-Miranda greeted the old man.

Charlie looked up and nodded. 'Good afternoon, miss.'

'I heard that you had quite a busy day,' Alice-Miranda continued.

'I think busy would be stating half the fact,' Charlie replied, his blue eyes twinkling. 'It's no wonder Reggie Parker prefers to sleep.'

Alice-Miranda grinned. 'People keep saying that. It's a pretty extreme way to avoid chores.'

Alice-Miranda was admiring the colours on an orchid sitting on Charlie's workbench when the telephone rang. The old man answered it and Alice-Miranda couldn't help but hear part of the conversation.

'Charlie Weatherly speaking . . . of course,

Miss Fayle, I can do that for you . . . I'll be over in ten minutes . . . Goodbye.' He placed the handset back into the cradle and turned to Alice-Miranda. 'It seems that one of your carnival friends has gone and got himself lost over at Caledonia Manor,' Charlie began. 'A boy. Tarquin, I think she called him.'

'Oh, poor Fern, she won't know where he is.' Alice-Miranda bit her lip. 'She'll be so worried.'

And then Alice-Miranda realised that this was a perfect opportunity.

'Mr Charles, I think I overheard that you're going to Caledonia Manor to pick up Tarquin and take him back to the camp,' she said. 'Do you think I could come too? And then on the way I can ask you the question I came about in the first place, and then I can find Fern too and apologise for what happened with Mrs Howard earlier.'

Charlie frowned, wondering what Alice-Miranda was talking about. 'What happened with Mrs Howard earlier?'

'It was just a misunderstanding but I would hate for Fern to think that Mrs Howard had accused her of something she didn't do,' Alice-Miranda explained. 'Please may I come with you? I can explain everything on the way and Tarquin might be quite happy to see me, seeing that we met yesterday.'

'Isn't he part of the reason you got the bump on your forehead?' Charlie asked cautiously.

'It wasn't his fault,' Alice-Miranda replied. 'And it's almost gone.'

'We should tell Howie,' Charlie advised. 'Do you want to run across and make sure that it's okay?'

'Mrs Howard is in the laundry with some of the other girls. I'm sure they won't have time to miss me.' This was true, but Alice-Miranda was reluctant to seek out her housemistress's approval, knowing how concerned she had been earlier about Fern being at the house.

'Well, I'll call and leave a message on the house phone instead,' Charlie decided.

'That's perfect,' Alice-Miranda nodded.

Alice-Miranda and Charlie drove around to the back of Caledonia Manor and found Hephzibah on the veranda with her young guest. Half a dozen cats clambered over him, smooching and generally vying for his attention.

'Hello Mr Weatherly,' Hephzibah called. 'Thank you for coming. I didn't know how to contact the boy's family and I'm sure they must be getting worried by now.'

Alice-Miranda exited the passenger door of the utility.

'Oh, hello dear,' Hephzibah added. 'I didn't know you'd be coming along too.'

'Hello Miss Hephzibah.' Alice-Miranda waved back at the old woman. 'I want to catch up with Fern when we take Tarquin home.'

Charlie and Hephzibah were soon engaged in a hushed conversation so Alice-Miranda went to see Tarquin.

'Hello Tarquin,' she said. He seemed mesmerised as he stroked the plush fur of a black-and-white cat. Alice-Miranda tried again. 'It's nice to see you.'

Tarquin looked up. He pointed towards the bandaid on her forehead.

'It's all right,' said Alice-Miranda.

'Come along, we'd better get moving if we're going to be back in time for tea,' Charlie called.

Alice-Miranda motioned for Tarquin to come with her. 'We need to get in the car.'

But Tarquin didn't budge.

'We have to go and find Fern. She'll be worried about you.'

Tarquin ignored her completely.

Alice-Miranda was worried that if they tried to force him, he might get upset.

She ran to where Hephzibah and Charlie were standing. She'd had an idea.

'If you think it will work, dear, I'm sure that puss will find his own way home,' Hephzibah offered.

Alice-Miranda ran back to Tarquin.

'Would you like to bring him along?' She pointed at the black-and-white cat in his lap. 'He can come with us in the car.'

Tarquin stood up and cuddled the cat to his chest. The animal seemed to have taken a shine to the boy and was nuzzling the side of his face.

'Say goodbye to Miss Hephzibah, Tarquin,' Alice-Miranda instructed the lad.

He looked over at the old woman and waved. 'Bye.'

Hephzibah smiled. 'Goodbye, Tarquin. Please come again.'

Tarquin, still holding the cat, followed Charlie and Alice-Miranda to the car.

★

Back at the camp, Fern had rallied a small group of adults and older children. Armed with torches, they were about to set off and look for her missing brother. He'd never spent a night out alone and she couldn't imagine how frightened he must be, out there in the forest with the light fading. Blasted Pete – he knew better than to tell Tarquin to get lost.

'Who's that?' One of the older boys pointed at the vehicle coming towards them over the rise.

As the car had bumped along the road through the forest, Tarquin remained focused on the cat on his lap. He stroked it and rubbed his face against it, and whispered in its ear. He couldn't have cared less where they were. But as the vehicle stopped, Fern ran towards the ute and wrenched open the door.

'Tarq, thank goodness you're all right.' She reached into the vehicle and pulled him from the seat, hugging him and the cat.

'Where have you been, boy?' Alf demanded as he strode over to the car.

Alice-Miranda slid across the seat and out the door.

'Hello – are you Mr Alf? My name is Alice-Miranda Highton-Smith-Kennington-Jones and it's lovely to meet you.' She walked towards the ginger-bearded man and held out her tiny hand.

Alf frowned and stared at her.

Alice-Miranda raised her eyebrows as if challenging the fellow to shake her hand, which strangely enough he did.

'When Millie and I met Fern and Tarquin and the other kids yesterday we heard about you. It sounds like you run a very good show, Mr Alf, and I for one can't wait until it's on. This is Mr Charles,' she finished, gesturing towards Charlie, who had walked around to the passenger side of the vehicle.

'Hello,' Alf grunted and reached out to shake Charlie's hand too.

'I think Tarquin must have wandered off earlier this afternoon and a friend of ours, Miss Hephzibah, found him in her garden. It was lucky that she did or he might have spent the night in the woods. Anyway, he's back now safe and sound,' Alice-Miranda explained.

'What's he doing with that cat?' Alf growled.

'It's one of Miss Hephzibah's,' Alice-Miranda replied. 'She's got quite a lot of them. When I first heard about her the girls at school told me that she had hundreds of them and that she was a witch, but of course none of that was true – well, she's not a witch and there aren't quite hundreds of cats, more like dozens. Miss Hephzibah thought Tarquin might like to have the cat keep him company on the way back over here.'

'Well, it's not staying,' Alf said, and shook his head.

'I want to keep him.' Tarquin clutched the feline closer to his chest. 'He's mine.'

'No, Tarquin, you can't.' Fern reached out and tried to take the creature from him.

Tarquin resisted. 'It's my cat. The lady with the burned face said I could keep him.'

Charlie intervened, motioning for Alf to step away from the group. 'Look, your boy there seems quite taken with the cat. Is there any chance you can let him keep it just for the next little while and then when you push off I can come and collect it?'

'I don't need another mouth to feed,' Alf hissed.

Charlie shrugged. 'I can't imagine you're going to have much fun if you take it away. He seems a bit of an unusual lad.'

Alf grunted. 'You're right about that. I suppose it won't hurt if the darn thing stays here for a few days but you'd better come and get him before we leave, or it'll be a bucket of water and a welding glove for that moggy.'

'That won't be necessary,' Charlie reproached.

The two men walked back to the children.

'You can keep the blasted cat for now, Tarquin,' Alf said. 'But don't get too attached – it's not staying forever.'

Alice-Miranda looked at Fern. 'Can I talk to you for a moment?' she asked.

'Why? So you can accuse me of stealing again,' the girl whispered.

'No, so I can explain what happened,' Alice-Miranda replied.

Fern whispered something to Tarquin and the boy headed off towards their caravan, clutching the cat in his arms. The girl turned her attention back to Alice-Miranda.

'Mrs Howard was just surprised to find you in the house,' Alice-Miranda explained. 'She's wary, that's all, and she'd had a difficult day at Mrs Parker's.'

'She's rude, more like it,' Fern retorted. 'I wasn't doing anything wrong. You told me I could have a look and that's all I did.'

'I believe you, Fern. And I'm so sorry – you still haven't had anyone look at your sore arm, have you?' Alice-Miranda asked.

'I'll live,' the amber-eyed girl said with a shrug.

'All right, you lot, nothing more to see,' Alf called out. The group began to disperse, some back towards the fire and others to their caravans.

'Please come over to school tomorrow afternoon so Mrs Howard can look at your wrist,' Alice-Miranda offered.

'Why do you care?' Fern asked. She'd never met anyone as persistent as this child.

'I thought we could be friends,' Alice-Miranda replied.

'Friends? Why would you want to be my friend?' Fern asked, her eyes locking with Alice-Miranda's.

'Fern, dinner won't cook itself,' Alf barked. 'Get yourself inside.'

'Goodbye, Mr Alf.' Alice-Miranda walked over and stood in front of the hairy man. 'It's been nice to meet you and I'm looking forward to the rides at the show.'

Alf didn't know what to say. He'd usually have given any child who dared to talk to him an earful for being a smart alec, but she was different, this one. Fern stepped closer, curious about the exchange.

'Goodbye Fern,' said Alice-Miranda, looking up at the older girl. 'Please come and see me tomorrow.'

Fern didn't say a thing.

'Ferny, that's not very friendly,' said Alf, his ears pricking up at Alice-Miranda's offer. 'Little girl wants you to pay her a visit – I'm sure that would be lovely for both of you.'

Fern wondered why Alf was so interested.

Then he winked and Fern gulped. She knew exactly what Alf meant by that comment and at that moment she hated him more than ever before.

Chapter 22

Late on Sunday afternoon, Ambrosia Headlington-Bear stood in the hallway of Wisteria Cottage wondering what she would tell her daughter. She had just arrived back in the village and felt as if her whole life had been snatched out from underneath her. The cottage was a shambles but at least it had a bed and hot and cold running water.

So much for thinking her husband had a special surprise for her. It had been more like a bombshell and certainly wasn't the dazzling diamond necklace she'd been hoping for. They'd had a lovely night at the ball. Ambrosia had worn her new Chanel frock and Neville looked as handsome as ever. They'd even danced, which was surprising seeing as her husband had never been especially fond of it. On the drive home they were chatting about this and that when, like a slap, he told her that their marriage was over. Just like that, with the same amount of emotion as if he'd told her he was heading off to golf or going to the gym.

Although they didn't spend a lot of time together, Neville had always seemed adoring. But for reasons he said he'd rather not share, he had decided to end their marriage. No conversation, no explanation, nothing. She thought he'd bought Wisteria Cottage as a weekend getaway, but Neville calmly explained that all her things would be delivered in the next week and she shouldn't return to the townhouse. The locks would be changed as soon as she left the next day.

As well as the house and the car, Ambrosia would receive a monthly allowance. She had told him it wouldn't pay the bill for her hairdresser and stylist, let alone her clothes. But Neville Headlington-Bear was not a man to trifle with. He told her that if she overspent she'd better start selling her jewellery. Wisteria Cottage was going to be her new home whether she liked it or not. And she had better start living within her means.

It wasn't in Ambrosia's nature to beg, but she wanted to make sure that the removalists packed everything that belonged to her. She dialled her husband's telephone number and waited.

'Hello Neville darling, please, don't hang up . . .' she began. Their conversation lasted only a few minutes and by the time it was over Ambrosia felt as if someone had punched her in the stomach. Her own husband had accused her of being a terrible mother. As if he was one to speak! He'd never shown any interest in their daughter; not from the moment she was born and the boy he'd been expecting had turned out to be a girl.

Ambrosia reached down and flicked the switch on a paint-spattered radio sitting on the floor. She turned up the volume, hoping that the noise would drown out her thoughts. Maybe a bath would help. At least that room was finished. Ambrosia walked through the master bedroom into her new ensuite, her sky-scraping heels clacking along the bare boards.

'Oh, gross!' She recoiled as she realised that the bath was covered in dust and would need to be cleaned before she got in it. She turned on the tap and a gush of rust-coloured water spewed out.

'But . . . I don't clean bathrooms.' A fat tear wobbled in the corner of her eye and spilled onto her cheek.

'Hellooo,' a shrill voice called from the back door. 'Is anyone home?'

The last thing Ambrosia felt like was visitors. She decided to ignore them.

'Helloooooo, I can hear you in there,' the woman called again.

Ambrosia turned off the tap and stalked down the hallway. She brushed the tears from her face and wrenched open the back door.

'Heavens be,' the woman screeched above the sound of the music. 'Are you deaf, dear?'

Ambrosia frowned at her.

'Turn off that dreadful noise,' the visitor demanded.

Ambrosia walked back up the hallway and turned the radio off.

'Thank the good Lord,' the woman yelled, before realising she was no longer competing with the ear-splitting racket. 'Well, aren't you going to invite me in?' Myrtle Parker peered through the gauze of the flyscreen door.

'I'm really not ready for visitors,' said Ambrosia. She wondered who she was talking to.

'Well dear, I think that's quite beside the point. I just wanted to say hello and welcome you to the neighbourhood, even though I'm so busy at the moment I can hardly spare the time.' Myrtle's voice had grown more querulous now. 'It's the neighbourly thing to do, isn't it?'

Ambrosia glanced around at the chaos. She was mortified that anyone should see her life in this state but she didn't want to get offside with the neighbours, especially not one as insistent as this.

'Oh all right, come in,' she sighed.

Myrtle Parker let herself in and walked into the kitchen, which had been stripped bare apart from the kitchen sink and one small cupboard. She then picked a path along the passageway, avoiding the tins of paint and other paraphernalia before arriving in the front sitting room.

'You must be Ambrosia Headlington-Bear,' Myrtle said.

Ambrosia nodded. 'Yes, yes I am. How did you know? I suppose you read *Gloss and Goss*?'

'No, dear, I'm not interested in that rubbish. Mr Munz told me that you were moving in. And I am sorry to hear about your husband,' Myrtle replied, casting her eyes to the floor as if there was some sort of embarrassment Ambrosia didn't yet know about.

'What about my husband?' Ambrosia certainly hadn't told anyone about their break-up. She wanted to time it exactly right before leaking the news to the press.

'I don't want to be the bearer of more bad news, dear,' said Myrtle smugly. 'I'm sure that you'll read about it sooner or later. Anyway, I'm Myrtle Parker and I live across the road. Perhaps you'd like to give me a quick tour?'

Ambrosia wondered what Mrs Parker was talking about. She tried to fob the woman off. 'I'm afraid the house is a complete mess. Perhaps we could do it next week, once the painters are gone and the kitchen is in.'

But Myrtle would not be dissuaded so easily. 'I've heard your ensuite is finished.'

Ambrosia nodded and said, 'But it hasn't been cleaned.'

'I don't mind about that, dear. I'm just interested to see what you've done to the place. Such a pretty cottage. Well, at least it was.'

Ambrosia glared at Mrs Parker before leading her through the master bedroom and into the ensuite.

Myrtle studied the space, with its glossy white wall tiles and expensive fittings. 'That's a pity, dear.'

'What do you mean?' Ambrosia asked.

'It's all white. Couldn't you afford any colour?' Myrtle wondered if the woman had any taste at all.

'Oh no, Mrs Parker, this is very up to the minute,' Ambrosia protested.

'For now, that is. Terribly dull, though,' Myrtle tutted.

Ambrosia considered her guest. Who was this woman, dressed as she was in the most frightful red gingham dress Ambrosia had seen in years, to tell her about style?

She could only imagine the bathroom in her house. It probably had an avocado suite.

'Wasn't this a bedroom?' Myrtle asked, remembering when Doris Foyle lived in the cottage. The room had housed the old woman's sewing machine and been a very handy little craft space.

'Yes, but as there's just me, I really couldn't

see the need for so many bedrooms,' Ambrosia replied.

'What about your daughter? Won't she be coming to stay with you?' Myrtle asked.

Mrs Parker certainly knew a lot about her, Ambrosia thought to herself.

'Yes, sometimes on the weekends, perhaps, but she loves her school,' Ambrosia replied. She stopped short of saying that she could hardly imagine Jacinta living with her permanently.

'But you do have a bedroom for her, I presume?' Myrtle spied another doorway. 'What's that through there?'

'It's my wardrobe and dressing room,' Ambrosia replied.

'Well, where's your daughter going to sleep when she comes?'

'She has a space.' Ambrosia was thinking about the tiny box room off the kitchen.

'I hope you're not thinking to put the poor child in that dreadful little room off the kitchen,' Myrtle gasped. 'Might as well put a cubbyhouse in the back garden and let her stay there – it would be an improvement.'

Ambrosia felt a twinge in her stomach. She

hadn't really considered that Jacinta might want to stay very often. It was only meant to be a weekender, after all.

'Anyway, I'd best be off.' Myrtle Parker's eyes scanned each room on her way down the hall. 'What sort of kitchen are you putting in?'

'It's white,' Ambrosia replied in a rebellious tone.

'I should have guessed.' Myrtle nodded, a superior smirk creeping across her face.

Myrtle turned to face Ambrosia and held out her hand. In it was a small envelope. 'It's an invitation to the show ball. But I'm afraid you'll have to pay. I can't afford to go around giving out free tickets.'

'Oh.' Ambrosia's mood improved at the thought of an invitation. And to a ball, no less. 'Where will it be held?' She wondered if it might be in the ballroom at Chesterfield Downs or on some other property she wasn't yet familiar with.

'It's in the village hall,' Myrtle replied. 'Beside the showground, next to the racetrack.'

'Oh.' Ambrosia's lip curled and she didn't even try to mask her disappointment. 'Really?'

'Yes. It's a fundraiser, Mrs Headlington-Bear. Probably not up to your usual standards but it's for a wonderful cause. I chose it myself this year. The money will go to an organisation called Coma Care, who look after people who are trapped in a permanent state of slumber, like my dear Reginald.' The old woman snapped open her handbag and pulled out a photograph, which she shoved towards Ambrosia.

'Who's that?'

'That's Reginald, in the front sitting room.' Myrtle stuffed the blurry picture back into her bag. 'He's been like it for three years now.'

'What? Asleep?' Ambrosia scoffed.

'Yes, Mrs Headlington-Bear. My dear Reginald has been in that state for far too long, and I fear that if he doesn't wake up soon, I am going to have to find someone to paint the outside of the house for him.' Myrtle sighed and silently wondered how much Ambrosia was paying her painters. 'Anyway, will you be coming to the ball or not? *Everyone* will be there.'

Ambrosia didn't feel quite so keen now she knew it would be in a hall, which was not much better than a shed, really. 'I'm not sure, Mrs Parker. I'll have to check my diary.'

'I suppose it won't interest you then that Queen Georgiana is planning to attend, in honour of this being the 150th continuous year of the show.'

'Oh, well, I'm sure I can cancel any other engagements. If Her Majesty is going to be there, of course I couldn't say no. We were just on a cruise together a couple of months ago, actually,' Ambrosia purred. She glanced at her fingernails and decided she should make a booking at the spa in Downsfordvale quick smart.

'So I can count on your support, Mrs Headlington-Bear?' Myrtle licked her lips and they smacked together noisily.

'Yes, of course. I wouldn't miss it for the world,' said Ambrosia.

'Very good then.' Myrtle raised her drawn-on eyebrows. 'I will see you the Saturday after next.' She waddled down the back steps into the garden, muttering under her breath, 'What a dreadful extravagance. Silly woman must have more money than sense.'

She walked down the driveway and crossed the street to enter her own ramshackle garden. Her thoughts drifted to Reginald and how thoroughly selfish it was of him to just lie there in the sitting room, especially when there were weeds to be tended and painting to be done. That woman across the road didn't know how lucky she was to be able to afford help.

Chapter 23

Alice-Miranda and Charlie had arrived back at school just in time for dinner. Despite being out of the school for most of the day, Mrs Smith had whipped up an enormous pot of bolognaise to serve with some delicious penne pasta and garlic bread hot from the ovens.

Millie, Jacinta and Sloane were already sitting together when Alice-Miranda made her way into the dining room.

The tiny child raised her nose in the air and drew in a deep breath. 'Yum, something smells delicious.'

'Where have you been?' Millie asked as Alice-Miranda sat down beside her.

The younger girl launched into a detailed account of the last couple of hours, finishing with, 'I'm rather hoping she'll come over tomorrow so Mrs Howard can take a look at her wrist.'

Millie snorted. 'I don't think Howie will be too happy about that.'

'We went to visit Granny Henrietta and Miss Hephzibah earlier,' Sloane interrupted, 'but we didn't see any boys.'

'Yeah, and as soon as we got back Howie had us folding washing for *hours*,' Jacinta griped.

'Tarquin must have shown up later,' Alice-Miranda told Sloane, before turning to Jacinta. 'Did you talk to your mother today?'

'No, but I tried. Her phone just kept going to voicemail,' Jacinta said.

'Oh,' Alice-Miranda said thoughtfully. 'Perhaps her phone's battery is flat.'

'I doubt it,' Jacinta replied. 'Her phone is like an extra body part.'

Over their delicious dinner, Alice-Miranda and Millie told the girls about their day. Millie finished up with the story of Mrs Howard scaring Fern from Grimthorpe House.

'I'm glad she did,' Sloane retorted. 'I don't want any sly carnival children hanging around my things.'

'Sloane, that's so unfair,' Alice-Miranda chided. 'You don't know her at all.'

'My point exactly, Alice-Miranda. You don't really know her either.'

'Oh, and don't get in a car with Billy Boots,' Millie warned.

'Why?' Jacinta asked.

'He gave us a lift over to Chesterfield Downs and he obviously thinks he's a racing car driver.' Millie's green eyes were huge as she recounted the terrifying ride. 'I think there's something a bit weird about him.'

Alice-Miranda opened her mouth to object, then closed it again. She hated to hear anyone being spoken of unkindly, but even she was beginning to have her doubts about Billy Boots. It was nothing she could say for sure, just a feeling that there was more to that young man's story than he was prepared to tell.

Chapter 24

On Monday morning after breakfast, Millie and Alice-Miranda were on their way to class when they noticed Mrs Smith's Mini coming down the driveway with Billy Boots in the passenger seat. They waved to the pair as the car drove by.

'I wonder where they're off to,' said Millie. She didn't notice Charlie Weatherly pushing his wheelbarrow up behind them.

'Mrs Smith is taking the lad over to Myrtle Parker's place. He's going to help her with some odd jobs,' Charlie piped up. 'Then at least I'll know where he is all day.'

Alice-Miranda spun around. 'Oh, hello Mr Charles.'

'Really?' said Millie. 'Has he done something wrong?'

'Not exactly. He does a very good job, but he's always disappearing,' Charlie explained. 'I don't know where he goes. It's a mystery.'

'He's good at sneaking up on people too,' Millie said. 'I call him the phantom.'

'Ha! I thought that myself,' Charlie chortled. 'Well, he's going to be kept busy today.'

'Doing odd jobs for Mrs Parker sounds like a pretty bad punishment if you ask me. He's likely to lose his ears, you know.'

Alice-Miranda giggled.

'And why exactly is that?' Charlie asked, grinning.

'Because by the time he's finished, Mrs Parker will have chewed them off,' Millie replied.

'Better him than me.' Charlie winked and headed off towards the front of the school.

The two friends parted company as Millie had a music lesson and Alice-Miranda was off to PE. They were planning to see Mrs Derby at lunchtime to get their entries for the show finalised.

Mrs Smith pulled up outside Mrs Parker's overgrown bungalow and Billy hopped out.

'You'll have to find your own way back, I'm afraid. I have a lot on today,' Mrs Smith told him.

'I'll be right,' Billy said, and thanked her for the lift.

The lawn was a patchwork of weeds. When Billy had asked Charlie what sort of jobs he'd be doing, he didn't mention anything about gardening.

The front door opened and a sturdy woman wearing what appeared to be a floral housecoat appeared.

'Come along, young man, I don't have all day,' Myrtle called out.

He skipped up the steps two at a time. 'Hello Mrs Parker.'

'I'm glad to see you have plenty of energy, Mr Boots,' said Myrtle, looking him up and down. 'But I was expecting you a little earlier.' The old woman's lips drew together as if she had been sucking a lemon.

'I'm sorry. Charlie told me to come at nine,' said Billy. 'What exactly would you like me to do?'

'Follow me.' Myrtle led the way into the small foyer and towards the kitchen.

Through a doorway, Billy glimpsed a man lying in a hospital bed in the middle of a sitting room. A woman in a nurse's uniform was administering some kind of medication through a tube.

'Don't mind Reginald,' said Myrtle. 'He won't be any trouble at all. But I have to warn you, if he doesn't like what you've done, I'm afraid you won't be getting paid.'

The nurse looked up and smiled at Billy, then rolled her eyes as if they were both in on the same joke.

Billy frowned. The man didn't seem to be conscious, much less capable of assessing his handiwork.

In the kitchen Myrtle presented Billy with a list, itemised in order of priority.

1. Clean out gutters
2. Attend to cobwebs
3. Wash awnings
4. Oil garden furniture

5. Fix broken tiles on roof . . .

Billy read on to the last point:

30. Wash and polish car

Billy wondered if she expected him to get everything done in just one day.

'I want you to do the jobs in order, young man, and understand that I will be watching you closely. Charles Weatherly told me that you're a capable lad, but I need to see that for myself,' Myrtle bleated.

Billy sighed. 'Do you have a ladder, Mrs Parker?'

'It's in the garage. Just make sure that you don't fall off. That's what happened to my Reginald, you know.'

'Oh,' Billy gulped.

True to her word, Myrtle Parker spent the first hour watching Billy like a hawk. She didn't offer to help at any time but she had plenty of advice. In between her telling him how to do this and that she regaled Billy with the story of her husband's accident, which the young fellow responded to with the appropriate responses of 'oh, no' and 'that's awful'.

'Where are you from?' she asked.

'Up north,' Billy said vaguely.

'Where up north?'

'Around Cossington Park,' Billy replied.

'Really? My Reginald was from Cossington Park,' said Myrtle. 'I bet you must know the Wrights and the Figworths. And dear old Della French.'

Billy had no idea who she was talking about but he had the good sense to nod and pretend that he did.

'You must be from fine stock then, Mr Boots,' Myrtle decided. 'Do you know much about the people here in the village?'

'No, not really,' Billy replied.

'Well then, I'll give you a quick potted history so you know who you're dealing with.' Myrtle pursed her lips. 'It's a lovely little place, really, but you must be careful about the gossips.'

Billy grinned to himself. Geez, that would be the pot calling the kettle black, he thought.

'Herman Munz is the grocer. Lovely man. Wife is terribly bossy, she's Marta. They have a son Otto who is a complete dunderhead. Never trust the boy to deliver your groceries. By the time he gets them to you your milk will be sour and your bread crustier than a school boy's scabby knees.' Myrtle continued reeling off her list. 'And I suppose you know quite a bit about those who work at the school. Ophelia Grimm's the headmistress. She was such a pretty young thing. Had a tragic time earlier on but I think she and Aldous Grump are happy enough now. Doreen Smith's the cook. Lovely woman too – husband died of a heart attack many years ago. She and I have such a bond, although I must say she's been getting a little bossy in her old age.' Myrtle cast her eyes towards the sitting room. 'And my new neighbour across the road . . . You've probably seen her daughter up there at the school. Ambrosia Headlington-Bear is quite the party girl – beautiful woman but terribly full of her own importance. Perhaps her marriage break-up will bring her down a few rungs on that social ladder she likes to climb. I read that her husband had filed for divorce – it was strange but she didn't seem to know anything about it – poor dear. But you didn't hear any of this from me.' Myrtle finally paused to take a breath.

Billy was wondering if there was anything she didn't know about the people who lived around the village, when she began again.

'Then there's Evelyn Pepper up at Chesterfield

Downs. Clever woman but frightfully too focused on her career. No time for anything or anyone unless they have four legs. Beautiful place, Chesterfield Downs. Have you been? No, of course you haven't.'

'I was there just yesterday,' Billy advised.

Myrtle was startled. 'Really? Whatever for?'

'A couple of the girls from school needed a lift and as everyone else was busy, Charlie asked me to drive them.'

'Well, no doubt you'd have noticed how peculiar the place is. I mean, that house has one of the most valuable collections of silverware in the whole country but their security is appalling,' Myrtle tutted. 'Not an alarm in the place. But I suppose that's one of the joys of living in the country, isn't it? We're a community-minded lot, everyone looking out for everyone else. And we need to be doubly alert over the next couple of weeks with those carnival people about town. It's my greatest wish to have the show without all those dreadful rides and distractions but apparently my committee says it's the only way we attract the youngsters or make any money. Last year those carnival folk left town with a hoard of garden furniture and my dear Newton.'

'Who's Newton?' Billy asked. It wasn't a name that had come up before in their conversation.

'My gnome. He's a charming little character and *such* a comfort. Whenever I was in the garden I could always chat to Newton about Reginald. But last year he went missing the very night that the travellers went on their way.'

'Oh.' Billy wasn't sure how else he could respond to such a statement.

'The naughty fellow must have covered some miles this past year. Do you know, I received postcards from all over the countryside from him and then just the other day, who should arrive back on my doorstep?'

There was a short silence. Billy didn't know what to say, given that the old woman seemed to believe that her garden gnome was actually capable of writing postcards and travelling about the country.

'Don't you want to guess?' said Myrtle. She was starting to wonder if the lad was a little on the slow side.

'Newton?' Billy offered.

'Of course it was Newton!' Myrtle clasped her hands together in delight. 'Little monkey was none the worse for wear but I've made sure that he stays inside these days. You never know when he might get the wanders again.'

'But you don't think he just went off on his *own*, do you, Mrs Parker?' Billy simply had to ask.

'Good gracious, no,' Myrtle replied. 'He had accomplices and if I was a gambling woman, which of course I'm not, I'd put the house on the instigators being those carnival folk.'

Billy couldn't help but wonder if Mrs Parker was a little unstable.

Myrtle glanced at her watch. 'Heavens, I'd better get going. Are you almost finished?' she demanded.

'This is a very long list,' Billy replied as he brushed the last cobweb from the awning.

'Well, I suppose I can leave you here while I duck out. Did Charlie say when you have to be back at the school?' Myrtle asked.

Billy hesitated, before saying truthfully, 'He said that I should stay until I get everything done.' He didn't say that Charlie told him to do everything in his power to make Myrtle Parker happy. Knowing her a little bit now, the lad thought he'd be there for weeks to make that happen.

'You'd better put that away in the garage,' the old woman said, pointing at the ladder.

Billy sighed. It was no wonder her husband preferred to be asleep. He carried the ladder to the garage and made sure that there was nothing else lying about.

'Now, I've thought of a few more things to add to the list.' Myrtle appeared with another piece of paper on which was written at least ten new jobs.

Billy worked as quickly as he could to get everything done. Without Mrs Parker chewing his ears off, he found that he got through things far more quickly. By the time she arrived home several hours later he'd almost finished.

'Take me through everything, young man,' Myrtle demanded. 'And don't try to get away with anything. I have keen eyes.'

Myrtle Parker inspected each job microscopically.

'Yes well, you seem to have done rather well. Except for the garden. I suppose it will just have to wait until next time.'

Billy hoped there wouldn't be a next time. That garden would take weeks to get under control.

'Come along, then.' Myrtle headed to the

kitchen, where she proceeded to pull a large teapot from the bottom cupboard.

Billy followed. 'Thanks, Mrs Parker, but I don't have time for tea.'

'I wasn't about to make you any,' Myrtle scoffed. She lifted the lid and to the young man's surprise the pot contained rolls and rolls of bank notes – all large denominations.

'I don't trust the banks,' Myrtle said. 'Now, how much do I owe you for today?'

Billy told her an amount, to which Myrtle added a very stingy tip.

'Well, you'd better hurry along,' the old woman instructed. 'I'm sure there are jobs waiting at the school and they won't do themselves.'

Chapter 25

Alice-Miranda had kept an eye out all day for Fern. She wished the young girl would come back and let Mrs Howard look at her wrist, but she wasn't entirely hopeful. Fern hadn't seemed all that keen, even with Alf's encouragement, and Mrs Howard could be rather stern when she wanted to be. If that was the side of the housemistress Fern had encountered, then the girl wasn't likely to venture anywhere near Grimthorpe House any time soon. Alice-Miranda wasn't sure when she would have time to go and see Fern again either.

At lunchtime Alice-Miranda and Millie had visited Mrs Derby to finalise their entries for the show. The headmistress's assistant had been busy all day collecting the last forms and said that she would drive them over to the Show Society office at 3 pm and hand them to Myrtle Parker herself. She joked that she might have someone photograph the exchange for insurance. The deadline was 4 pm and there was no way the girls were going to miss out.

Alice-Miranda had arranged a lift with Mrs Smith to Chesterfield Downs for Tuesday and Thursday afternoons. On Monday Alice-Miranda had hockey practice and on Wednesday there was choir rehearsal. On Friday Mrs Smith was busy with another committee meeting, so Alice-Miranda thought she could have an afternoon off. Millie would train Chops at school until the weekend, when there would be time to ride over and practise together again.

Alice-Miranda and Millie were walking back to the house from hockey practice when they spotted a police car making its way up the driveway. It stopped near the visitors' parking lot and Billy Boots hopped out of the passenger's seat.

'Thanks,' Billy said with a wave.

Constable Derby put the window down and called out, 'You will let me know if you see anything then?'

'Course,' Billy replied and walked towards the manor.

The police car made its way around the turning circle in front of the building and headed back down the driveway.

Billy hadn't seen Millie and Alice-Miranda standing near the steps.

'Hello Mr Boots,' Alice-Miranda said as she and Millie appeared from behind the hedge. Billy jumped.

'You surprised the life out of me,' he complained, wondering where she had come from.

'Ha!' Millie replied. 'Now you know how we feel every time you do it to us – phantom. I thought you didn't like policemen.'

'I don't but he offered me a lift and I didn't feel much like walking after all the jobs I've done today,' Billy answered.

'He's a lovely man, isn't he?' said Alice-Miranda.

'He seems all right,' Billy replied, 'for a copper.'

'Why was Constable Derby asking you to let him know if you see anything?' Millie asked.

Billy shot Millie a curious look. 'Well, don't you just have a pair of elephant ears on you.'

Millie rolled her eyes. 'He yelled it out to you. It didn't seem to be a secret.'

'It's nothing really – a bit of a joke. Apparently there's been some thieving going on around the village and he asked me to keep an eye out for anything suspicious,' Billy explained.

Millie glanced at Alice-Miranda. 'Mrs Parker's right, you know. There's always trouble when they come to town.'

'I thought you were going to give them a chance,' Alice-Miranda said, frowning at her friend.

'Well, if it's them, they're not very ambitious,' Billy replied. 'But Mrs Parker would know. She's got everyone in the village pegged. She spent an hour telling me everyone's business, including about some woman who's just moved into the cottage across the road. Ambrosia something or other. And then she invited me to a ball!' Billy shook his head in amazement.

'That's wonderful. I can't wait for the ball,' Alice-Miranda said excitedly. 'Everyone's going.'

Millie gave Alice-Miranda a sneaky smile. 'What did Mrs Parker say about Ambrosia?'

'That she's some society princess and her husband's divorcing her. Mrs Parker didn't think village life would suit her very well.'

Millie's smile dropped and she gulped as Alice-Miranda stared at her in shock.

'Do you think that could be true?' Millie asked.

'I suppose anything's possible,' Alice-Miranda replied. She looked at Billy Boots. 'I think it's best not to repeat anything Mrs Parker says. I'm sure that she gets things wrong sometimes.'

'I think you're right there.' Billy smiled, saluted the girls with his forefinger, then strode off towards the stables.

'Poor Jacinta,' Millie said. 'I wonder if she knows about her parents.'

'I doubt it,' Alice-Miranda replied, hoping that Ambrosia would at least tell her daughter herself instead of letting Jacinta find out from some awful magazine article.

Millie opened the front door and the two girls walked down the hallway to their bedroom. Jacinta and Sloane's door was open and the sound of laughter was coming from within the room.

Alice-Miranda poked her head inside and Millie followed.

'Hello,' Alice-Miranda said.

'Oh, hi Alice-Miranda,' Sloane replied. 'Hi Millie.' She was lying on her bed with her feet pointed in the air and Jacinta was on her bed doing the same thing.

'We're turtles.' Jacinta burst out laughing and swivelled around on her bed, flailing her arms and legs in the air. 'Upside down, of course.'

Alice-Miranda giggled. 'Why?'

'We were at drama and Miss Reedy did this activity where she would say an animal and then we had to be it, but when she said turtle that's what I did and everyone thought it was hilarious, so we've been practising some more for next week.'

'I know, I know,' said Sloane, still laughing. 'I'm a cockroach.'

Millie shook her head. 'You're both crazy.'

'You should try it, Millie,' Sloane suggested. 'It's fun.'

'I'll take your word for it,' Millie replied.

Jacinta rolled over. 'Hey, did you hear that there were some robberies in the village today?'

'What's been stolen?' Millie asked. 'Billy Boots mentioned something when we were walking back up to the house but he didn't give us any details.'

'Howie's been in a right flap because apparently Mr Munz had a whole box of chocolate bars disappear from the shop.' Sloane rolled over and propped her hands under her chin.

Millie put her hands on her hips. 'Chocolate bars? Is that all?'

'And Mrs Parker's favourite gnome has come home,' Jacinta said.

'So a box of chocolate bars has gone missing and a missing garden gnome has been found. It's hardly time to call in the sniffer dogs,' Millie giggled. 'Otto Munz is probably sitting in the woods stuffing his fat face as we speak. Everyone knows he loves sweets and his mother has put him on a diet. And whoever took that garden gnome clearly did it as a joke. Anyway, I feel sorry for the gnome. He was probably having a great time tripping around the place and now the poor thing's back with Mrs Parker.'

'I think you're wrong, Millie. You wait. The chocolate will be just the start. It always is when the show's on,' Jacinta replied.

'I'm not accusing Otto but really Millie's quite right – it's just as likely to be some local kids who know that every year when the show comes to town they can go on a little spree and never be caught because the poor children from the carnival will get the blame. I think it's terrible,' Alice-Miranda said decidedly.

'No, first it will be sweets, then anything else that's not nailed down,' said Jacinta.

Sloane agreed. Millie thought about it. Maybe Alice-Miranda was right.

Chapter 26

Alice-Miranda couldn't believe how quickly time whizzed by. In what seemed like the blink of an eye, it was already the weekend. The whole school was buzzing about the show and everyone seemed to be busy getting ready for this and that. Susannah had baked a cake every night for a week, testing different recipes and trying to work out which one would be just right. Of course she had no shortage of willing tasters. Millie was heard loudly complaining that her jodhpurs were getting so tight she'd have to buy a new pair before the show.

Ashima and Ivory were busy perfecting their blackberry jam recipe too. The first batch proved to be somewhat of a disaster when they used salt instead of sugar. And even the teachers were getting in on the act. Miss Wall was apparently an expert at needlepoint, and was seen in the back row of assembly finishing her handiwork. Mr Plumpton brought some giant vegetables in for the girls and Miss Reedy to admire. Even Miss Grimm had been inspired to finish a watercolour painting she'd started months ago.

As they had agreed, Mrs Smith had driven Alice-Miranda over to Chesterfield Downs on Tuesday and Thursday so she and Bony could train. Mrs Smith was baking for the lads over there each day and made sure that she timed her run to take Alice-Miranda with her. Alice-Miranda didn't have nearly as much fun riding alone, but there just wasn't enough time for Millie to walk Chops over to Chesterfield Downs in the afternoon. Millie was working him on the dressage arena near the stables at school instead.

Rockstar had made fantastic progress and he and Bony were getting on better than ever. Wally was having a ball riding track work and Miss Pepper had telephoned each day to get a progress report. Bonaparte only needed to stand beside the track and whinny and Rockstar seemed to get faster and faster.

On the weekend, Millie and Alice-Miranda had spent both mornings riding at Chesterfield Downs.

The carnival trucks had moved from Gertrude's Grove to the showground and on Sunday afternoon Alice-Miranda, Sloane, Millie and Jacinta decided to go for a walk into the village and see how it was all taking shape. Alice-Miranda was rather keen to find Fern too. She had hoped to see her during the week but the girl had apparently acquired powers of invisibility since the previous weekend.

Alice-Miranda and her friends walked around the perimeter of the showground looking at the rides in their various stages of construction. A mass of metal structures and worn signs were spread around the ground. Men worked all over the contraptions with wrenches and drills, putting pieces together and pulling some apart.

'Oh cool, I love that ride,' Sloane said as they passed a somewhat battered-looking machine with eight metal arms. The dented carriages were sitting beside it on the ground.

Jacinta curled her lip. 'Looks a bit dodgy to me.'

'My favourite is the pirate ship, over there.' Millie was admiring what really amounted to a giant swing with a rather suspect-looking ship attached to the sides.

'Look! Isn't that a gorgeous carousel?' Alice-Miranda called to the girls as she raced ahead. It truly was the showpiece of the carnival. A chubby girl with mousy hair tied in two bunches was sitting on top of one of the beautifully restored horses while a man Alice-Miranda assumed must be her father hammered away further around the circle.

'Hello Ivy,' Alice-Miranda said to the girl. 'Is that *your* carousel?'

'Yup. It's ours and it's the best thing here,' the child replied.

'It must be fun living in a carnival,' Alice-Miranda said.

'It's okay.' The child slipped down off the horse and jumped from the platform onto the ground. 'Have you got any chocolate?'

'No, I'm sorry,' Alice-Miranda answered.

Ivy looked annoyed.

Millie, Jacinta and Sloane had finally caught up.

'These are my friends. Do you remember Millie? And that's Jacinta and Sloane.' Alice-Miranda pointed to her friends in turn.

Ivy waved. 'Hi.'

'Ivy, do you know where Fern and Tarquin are?' Alice-Miranda asked.

She shook her head. 'No. They're probably doing jobs for Alf.'

'What sort of jobs?' Millie asked.

'I don't know.' Ivy stuck out her lip. 'Just the stuff that the big kids have to do.'

'Where are Fern's parents?' Alice-Miranda asked.

'Her mother's in the graveyard,' said Ivy.

'Oh,' Alice-Miranda said sadly. 'What about her father?' Alice-Miranda had begun to wonder if perhaps Alf was Fern and Tarquin's dad.

'She hasn't got one, except for Alf. That's what my mum says and she knows everything.'

'Well, if you do see Fern, could you please tell her that we were here?' Alice-Miranda looked at her friends. Jacinta was pulling on Sloane's arm and giving Alice-Miranda a 'hurry up' look.

'If you bring me some chocolate when the show's on, I'll let you have a ride for nothing,' the girl offered. 'But don't tell my mum or dad.'

Millie and Alice-Miranda exchanged grins. 'It's a deal.'

'Bye Ivy,' the girls chorused, waving as they walked away.

'Bye,' the child called.

'She's special,' said Jacinta, once the girls were out of earshot.

'Jacinta, that's unkind,' Alice-Miranda rebuked. 'But I wonder if what she said about Fern and Tarquin's mother was true?'

Millie could almost hear Alice-Miranda's over-active brain ticking away. 'What are you thinking now?'

Alice-Miranda frowned. 'Nothing, really. I . . . I don't know.'

The girls walked out of the showground and into the village, where they stopped at Mr Munz's shop to buy some ice-creams.

While the girls were crowding over the freezer, the shop bell tinkled. Jacinta looked up and spotted Lucas and Sep coming through the door. 'Hi there,' she called out.

'Oh, hi.' Lucas grinned and approached the group.

'I thought you were on camp again this weekend,' said Sloane.

'No, we have another one the weekend after the show,' said Sep.

'What have you been doing?' Lucas asked the girls.

'We went for a walk around the showground,' Millie said. 'Alice-Miranda's been making some new friends.'

'Of course she has.' Lucas smiled at his younger cousin. 'Hey, I heard it was your birthday the other week. What are you now? Twenty-six?'

'Ha ha, Lucas,' Alice-Miranda replied. 'I'm eight.'

'Yeah, a twenty-six-year-old trapped in the body of an eight-year-old,' he teased.

'Are you entering any events at the show?' Jacinta asked.

'Sep here will be playing the bagpipes,' said Lucas, slapping his friend on the back. 'And I'm going to set a new record for the most number of rides.'

'And he's entering a painting in the art show,' Sep added. 'It's really good. Who'd have thought – handsome and talented.'

'Me!' Jacinta sighed.

The rest of the group laughed.

'Are you kids buying ice-creams or having

conference up there?' Herman Munz called. 'I am busy man. Hurry up.'

'Busy watching *Winners Are Grinners*, more like it,' Sloane whispered.

The kids selected their treats and hurried to the counter where the *Winners Are Grinners* theme song blared out of the ancient television set on the end of the counter. Otto Munz was standing next to his father and rang the items through the till.

Outside, the children peeled the wrappers from their ice-creams and deposited them in the bin.

'We'd better go or Professor Winterbottom will send a search party,' Sep said.

'See you on Friday at the show,' Alice-Miranda said.

'Yeah, see you then,' Lucas and Sep chorused before heading off towards Fayle on the other side of the village.

On their way back to school, the girls had to walk past the church and its little graveyard. Sloane took a deep breath and held it in as they reached the boundary.

'Can we have a look inside?' Alice-Miranda asked, pointing at the gate.

Sloane exhaled. 'I thought you were supposed to

hold your breath when you walked past the cemetery. It keeps the evil spirits out.'

'That's just a silly old wives' tale,' Millie said. 'You might make it past a small cemetery like this one okay but imagine trying to do that if you were walking past some of the giant ones in the city. If you held your breath that long, the cemetery's where you'd end up.'

'Come on, we'll go with you to the cemetery,' said Jacinta. 'But only if you come with me to Wisteria Cottage afterwards. It's just down Rosebud Lane, and seeing as my mother hasn't been anywhere near me this week, I think I'd better go and look for myself or the lease will be up and I'll never have been there. I've been wondering if it's all a figment of Mother's overactive imagination anyway.'

Alice-Miranda reached out and slipped her hand into Jacinta's. 'Your mother's probably been very busy, that's all.'

'I don't know why you're always defending her, Alice-Miranda. I thought she might be getting better, but you know what they say, leopards really don't change their spots,' Jacinta frowned.

'But you've changed heaps, Jacinta. Don't you remember when we used to call you the school's second best tantrum thrower?' Millie reminded her.

'That's different,' Jacinta said, with narrowed eyes.

'I don't see how,' Millie argued.

Sloane looked like she wanted to say something too but thought better of it.

'Come on,' Alice-Miranda urged. 'We'd better get going.'

The group crossed the road and entered the churchyard. They took the path that led to the cemetery at the side of the church.

'Look,' Millie called out. 'Here's a Weatherly. "Thomas Charles Weatherly late of Winchesterfield-Downsfordvale". That must be Charlie's father who was the gardener at school before him.'

'And here's a Smith,' Jacinta called out. 'I wonder if he was Mrs Smith's husband.'

While her friends were studying the headstones, Alice-Miranda walked to the back of the plot to the newer graves. Mostly marked by shiny marble monuments, these were the most recently deceased members of their small community. But one stood out because of its small timber cross.

Alice-Miranda stopped to read the inscription. '"Gina Sharlan 1966–2011." I wonder why they haven't put a proper headstone on her grave. She's been gone for a little while,' Alice-Miranda noted.

Millie caught up to her friend. 'Sharlan, I've seen that name before somewhere. Oh, I know! It was on the side of one of the caravans at Gertrude's Grove. Sharlan's Carnival.'

'Of course,' Alice-Miranda said. 'Tarquin said that his full name was Tarquin James Sharlan. I wonder if what Ivy said was true then. Maybe Gina was Fern and Tarquin's mother,' Alice-Miranda said.

'Come on,' Jacinta yelled. 'I've had enough of all these dead people and if we don't go to the cottage now it will be too late.'

Millie gave Alice-Miranda an exasperated smile. She grabbed her friend by the hand and the two girls ran through the maze of headstones to the gate.

Chapter 27

Jacinta and Sloane led the way along Rosebud Lane. It was a pretty street with quaint cottages and the odd post-war bungalow dotted between, noticeable for their plain Jane looks. Wisteria Cottage was so named for the giant purple plant that had wrapped its tendrils around the veranda posts at the front of the house, lending shade and colour to the attractive facade.

The property opposite had none of the same charm. It was so overgrown with weeds that the house could hardly be seen.

'Well, this is it,' Jacinta said as they arrived at the gate. 'Mummy said that there's a key around the back.'

The girls followed their friend across the lawn to the driveway where Jacinta stopped suddenly.

'She's here.' Jacinta pointed at her mother's shiny sports car parked beside the house, far enough back that you couldn't see if from the road. 'I can't believe it!' she fumed.

Alice-Miranda gave her friend a worried look. 'Don't be upset, Jacinta,' she urged. 'Perhaps she's just arrived and was planning to come and visit you in a little while.'

'Really? We'll see about that.' Jacinta stormed around to the back veranda and raced up the steps. 'Mother! Where are you, Mother?'

The tall girl barged her way through the screen door into a gleaming new kitchen. While the outside of the cottage was clearly in need of further renovation, the inside was breathtaking.

'Mother? I know you're here somewhere!' Jacinta flew down the hallway with Alice-Miranda, Millie and Sloane close behind.

'Hello, Mrs Headlington-Bear,' Alice-Miranda called, trying to soften Jacinta's impending attack.

Jacinta stormed in and out of the rooms along the main hall until she finally found her mother. Ambrosia Headlington-Bear was sitting on the floor in the master bedroom amid a veritable warehouse of clothes and shoes, sobbing her heart out.

The woman looked up. 'What are you doing here, Jacinta?' Mascara trails lined her face and the white dress she was holding was streaked with black.

'You told me I could come and see the cottage. I haven't heard from you all week so I didn't think you were here,' Jacinta snapped.

'I was hoping it would be finished and you'd get a lovely surprise,' her mother sniffed. 'But now that's ruined too.' She began to bawl again.

'What do you mean, ruined *too*?' Jacinta looked around and wondered why her mother had brought so many clothes to a house that was only a week-ender. 'I don't understand why you're making Daddy spend so much money on a place that you're renting, either,' Jacinta fumed. 'You could feed half of Africa for all the money you spend on stupid things.'

Ambrosia's sobs finally died down and she regained some composure. 'I'm not renting the cottage, Jacinta.'

'Well, I'm not surprised,' Jacinta spat back at

her. 'I knew it wouldn't last. This whole act, that you actually care about me and you want to spend time here. You're just a big fat fake, Mother!'

'Jacinta!' Ambrosia squeaked. 'That's not it at all. I'm not *renting* the cottage because your father *bought* it.'

'Why? You hate the countryside and you've only been here a couple of times in the months you've had it.'

'I've been trying to get it renovated so you'd have somewhere nice to come and stay on the weekends.' Ambrosia's lip trembled as she spoke. After Mrs Parker's visit earlier in the week, Ambrosia had decided to make some further modifications to ensure there was a proper bedroom for her daughter.

'You just don't get it, Mother. I don't care about the house. I just wanted to spend time with you,' Jacinta fumed.

'Oh Jacinta, darling, there's so much to explain.' Ambrosia stood up and rushed towards her daughter. 'Things aren't the same as they used to be. They'll never be the same again.'

At this point Alice-Miranda directed Sloane and Millie to back out of the room.

'I think we should give them some privacy to sort things out,' the younger girl whispered as she led the other two down the corridor towards the back of the house. 'We should go back to school. I'm sure that Mrs Headlington-Bear will bring Jacinta back later once they've had time to talk.'

Alice-Miranda and her friends walked out to the road.

'What do you think is going on with Mrs Headlington-Bear?' Sloane asked.

'I'm not sure,' Alice-Miranda replied. 'Sometimes grown-ups are very complicated.'

Across the street Myrtle Parker had just arrived home and was complaining loudly to herself about having to lug the groceries from the boot of her car to the house.

Myrtle heard the children and swivelled around. She spotted them before the girls saw her.

'Alice-Miranda, what are you doing here?' she called.

'Oh, hello Mrs Parker.' The tiny child skipped across the road to her.

Millie groaned and rolled her eyes. 'I forgot that

Nosey lived in this street,' she whispered to Sloane. 'Just pretend we haven't seen her.'

'Millicent, have you lost something?' Myrtle called, tutting to herself about the lack of manners in children these days.

'No, Mrs Parker.' Millie dragged her feet across the road, with Sloane beside her.

'What a busy day I've had. Honestly, I don't know why I bother having a committee. It's really a committee of one. I do all of the work and I can tell you, girls, that I will have all of the glory when this show is proclaimed the best in the history of the village,' Myrtle prattled on.

'Mrs Smith's been very busy baking and I know Mrs Howard's had lots of jobs on her plate too and Mr Charles has been making sure that the orchids are perfect,' Alice-Miranda replied. 'I'm sure that your co-committee members are working very hard.'

'Yes, well, I imagine they've had loads of help from all the girls over at the school. I, on the other hand, am completely on my own. Worse than on my own, actually, with poor Reginald in there, in that state,' she said, pointing towards the front of the house.

'Millie told me about your husband, Mrs Parker. I am sorry,' said Alice-Miranda.

'You know, I talk to him constantly and play his favourite music and wear his favourite perfumes and it hasn't worked at all,' Myrtle sighed.

'I'd love to meet him. Perhaps I could come and read to Mr Parker,' the child suggested. 'This week's a little busy getting ready for the show, but after that's over I promise I would love to come at least twice a week, if I may.'

Myrtle Parker looked at the child, shocked. She rearranged her shoulders and sniffed, 'Well, if you can rouse my husband from his state of slumber I'll be very surprised.' She wondered if Alice-Miranda was serious or just pretending to be kind. 'Once you make a commitment I expect you to see it through, young lady.'

'Of course, Mrs Parker,' Alice-Miranda nodded.

Millie groaned and put her palm against her forehead.

'She has no idea what she's just done,' Millie whispered to Sloane.

Myrtle looked at the blonde girl. 'You're Sloane Sykes.'

Sloane nodded.

'Your grandmother is doing terribly well these days, no thanks to your mother or you. I've been there for her every step of the way – sweet woman that she is,' Myrtle admonished Sloane.

For once Sloane had no response at all.

'Now, girls, I hope you're keeping an eye out for anything suspicious going on around the village. The carnival folk have come to town and I think we all know what that means.' Myrtle tapped her fingertip to the side of her nose.

'I'm afraid I don't. What does it mean?' Alice-Miranda asked.

'Hijinks, chaos, pandemonium and things going missing.' Myrtle nodded emphatically.

Alice-Miranda looked the woman square in the eye. 'I don't think it's fair to accuse people when you have no proof, Mrs Parker.'

But Myrtle could not be swayed so easily. 'I don't need proof. They're just the sort, that's all.'

'I've met some of the carnival children and I think they're perfectly lovely,' Alice-Miranda replied.

'Really? Well, I think you should be careful. You're getting mixed up with a bad lot,' Myrtle scoffed.

Alice-Miranda bit her tongue for a moment, then said, 'Would you like some help with your groceries?'

Millie pulled a face and made a cutting motion across her neck.

'What was that, Millicent? I'm sure that I heard you offer to take this for me.' Myrtle handed Millie a heavy grocery bag. 'Don't worry, Sloane. You won't miss out. I've got plenty for everyone.'

The girls had two bags each while somehow Myrtle managed to carry nothing more than her handbag. She led the girls up the steps to the front porch and turned her key in the door.

'Helloooo, Reginald, I'm home,' she called. Myrtle walked through the front sitting room, where her husband lay on his hospital bed. 'Raylene, where are you?' Myrtle called to the nurse, who was supposed to be looking after Reginald. 'Honestly, that woman gets more and more unreliable every day.'

Alice-Miranda, Millie and Sloane stopped to look at Mr Parker. Except for all of the tubes and cables he was hooked up to, he looked like he was having a snooze.

'Come along, girls, you'll need to unpack those groceries,' Myrtle called.

A woman dressed in a nurse's uniform emerged from somewhere further inside the house.

'Raylene, where on earth have you been?' Myrtle chided her. 'I've told you not to leave Reginald alone when I'm away.'

'Can't I go to the loo?' Raylene asked.

'Don't get smart with me,' Myrtle snapped, 'or you'll be looking for another patient, toot sweet.'

Alice-Miranda introduced herself and her friends to the nurse in the usual way.

'Oh, for goodness sake, Raylene, get back in there and check on Reginald,' Myrtle interrupted. The woman skulked off into the sitting room.

Alice-Miranda, Millie and Sloane helped Mrs Parker unpack her groceries. It proved to be an exercise in military precision, with Mrs Parker barking orders. Millie glanced at the clock on the kitchen wall and tugged at Alice-Miranda's sleeve.

'We really must get going, Mrs Parker,' Alice-Miranda commented. 'We don't want to be late back to school.'

Myrtle was disappointed. She was thinking of some other jobs the girls could do. Her linen cupboard was in dire need of a tidy and truth be told she was quite enjoying having some young people in the house. 'Well, if you must. I'll see you all at the show on Friday. Good luck in your events. Although, Millie, please don't be disappointed if that pony of yours misses out on a ribbon. He's not exactly pedigree now, is he?'

'Maybe not, but at least he doesn't think he's anything special either,' said Millie, narrowing her eyes.

Myrtle Parker glared at the impertinent child. '*Well*. Hurry along, then.'

As the group followed Mrs Parker back through the sitting room, Alice-Miranda stopped and quickly introduced herself to Mr Parker.

'I'm looking forward to chatting with you soon,' she told him. 'I'd love to read you some of my favourite books. I just adore Roald Dahl. He's terribly clever and funny. I hope you do too.'

Alice-Miranda could have sworn she saw his eyelids flutter when she mentioned the author's name.

'Goodbye, Mr Parker. I'll be back to see you again soon.'

The girls bade farewell to Mrs Parker on the front veranda. Alice-Miranda volunteered a hug and was followed at Mrs Parker's insistence by Millie and Sloane. 'What did you have to hug her for, Alice-Miranda?' said Millie with a shudder as the girls walked down the lane towards the church.

'I think Mrs Parker needs lots of hugs,' the tiny child replied. 'I can't imagine how sad she must be with Mr Parker asleep in the sitting room.'

'Her house smells like mothballs,' Sloane added. 'I didn't know what to say to her after she made it clear that she thought I was the most horrid child in the world.'

'Well, I think I'm going to enjoy visiting Mr Parker,' Alice-Miranda said.

Sloane rolled her eyes. 'Alice-Miranda, sometimes you are just *not* normal.'

Chapter 28

Jacinta had arrived back at Grimthorpe House late on Sunday night with her mother. When Alice-Miranda and the girls got back they'd explained to Mrs Howard what had happened and Mrs Howard telephoned Ambrosia to let her know that it was fine for Jacinta to stay with her for the evening but Jacinta had wanted to come back to school and Ambrosia needed some time on her own to get things sorted out.

Monday had been a busy day and in the evening after dinner the girls had been enlisted to make signs for the show. The dining room was covered in cardboard and marker pens and the girls were having a wonderful time being creative.

'Is everything all right between you and your mother?' Alice-Miranda asked Jacinta quietly as they worked on a sign for the flower show.

'I suppose so. She's really needy and now I'm worried about her being here *all* the time. It's not much of a surprise though that Daddy has decided they should get a divorce – well, not to me, anyway. They've never liked each other all that much and my father has always been disappointed that I wasn't a boy. I just can't imagine Mother staying here forever though. The Village Women's Association won't exactly be her thing. But at least she finally told me the truth. I let her know how pathetic she was, sitting there in her bedroom bawling among the ball gowns.'

Alice-Miranda smiled at her friend. 'Don't be too hard on her, Jacinta. The break-up may have been quite a shock for your mother. I think she's lucky to have you so close now.'

'I suppose,' Jacinta shrugged.

At 8 pm Mrs Howard asked the girls to finish the signs they were working on and head back to the boarding house. The poor woman looked dead on her feet and she was worried that the girls would be late getting to bed.

On Tuesday night there was napkin folding duty and on Wednesday the girls made decorations for Mrs Smith's cafe, including a giant backdrop of a Parisian scene to hide the stage at the end of the pavilion. The excitement of the show was certainly building and all of the teachers were helping out too.

Alice-Miranda kept up her training at Chesterfield Downs and Mrs Smith kept up her baking. But on Thursday afternoon, when Mrs Smith picked Alice-Miranda up after her ride, instead of going straight back to school, she turned the Mini onto Downsford-vale Road and explained to Alice-Miranda that they were going to visit Miss Pepper. The girls were having a sausage sizzle for dinner back at school and Charlie and Billy were taking care of it, so it didn't matter if they were a little late getting home.

'I'm a terrible friend, Alice-Miranda,' Mrs Smith informed her young charge.

'Why do you say that?' the girl asked.

'I've only been to see Evelyn twice since she's been in hospital,' Mrs Smith sighed.

'But you've done all that baking for her boys and I know you've been talking to her on the telephone quite a lot,' Alice-Miranda pointed out. 'I'm sure Miss Pepper knows that you're a very good friend.'

Mrs Smith frowned. 'That's not what Myrtle Parker said. I know I'm just overreacting and I shouldn't let her get to me but that woman loves to make trouble.' Mrs Smith eased her foot off the accelerator as they reached the edge of the village.

She turned right into the hospital car park and drew into a spare spot.

'I wish I'd known we were coming,' Alice-Miranda said as they got out. 'I'd have asked Mr Charles for some flowers.'

'It's all right, dear.' Mrs Smith walked around to the back of the car and opened the tiny boot. 'He gave me these.' She pulled out a lovely bunch of roses with silver foil wrapped around the stems.

'They're gorgeous,' Alice-Miranda exclaimed.

Once inside the hospital, Mrs Smith led Alice-Miranda through a long ward to the room at the very end of the corridor. She poked her head around the door. 'Hello Ev, are you awake, dear?'

'Awake and bored out of my mind,' Evelyn Pepper replied.

Doreen Smith walked to the side of the bed and gave her friend a hug and kiss on the cheek. She handed her the roses.

'Oh, these are lovely!' Evelyn buried her nose into the centre of the blooms and sniffed. 'Charlie's handiwork, no doubt.'

Alice-Miranda stood beside Mrs Smith.

'Hello Miss Pepper. I hope you don't mind that I've come along. I was hoping to see you soon anyway. I'm . . .'

'Alice-Miranda Highton-Smith-Kennington-Jones,' Evelyn said. 'And I'm very glad that you came.'

'I wasn't sure if you'd remember me, Miss Pepper. I saw you earlier in the year when I was out riding my pony Bonaparte in the village,' Alice-Miranda said.

'Of course I remember you. I liked your pony too. He was a very sweet fellow,' Evelyn replied.

'I think you're one of the only people who would say that about Bony, other than me,' Alice-Miranda grinned. 'And maybe Mr Boots. Bonaparte really likes him for some reason too.'

'I feel as if I know you quite a bit already,' said Evelyn. She grimaced and shifted in the bed.

'Really?' Alice-Miranda asked, noticing the woman's discomfort. 'Why is that?'

'When Her Majesty was here last month, Dick and I were invited to dinner over at the house and she was regaling us with tales of your aunt's birthday party and her wedding on the *Octavia*. She had us in stitches,' Evelyn recalled. 'She has a wicked sense of humour.'

'Oh, we've have had a lot of fun with Aunty Gee this year,' Alice-Miranda confirmed. 'You should have seen her and Mrs Oliver when they took the speed boat out for a spin around the ship after the wedding. You would have thought they were both seventeen, not seventy.'

'Come and sit down.' Evelyn motioned at the two chairs either side of her bed. 'You two are making the place look untidy.'

'Is there anything I can get for you?' Mrs Smith asked.

Evelyn licked her lips. 'Actually, I'd love a cup of tea. I think there's one of those dreadful machines just down the hall. Have one with me, Dor.'

'I'll be right back. And you can tell Miss Pepper all about Rockstar's little romance with your Bonaparte,' Mrs Smith told Alice-Miranda before exiting the room.

'I think we'd call it a bromance,' Alice-Miranda said.

'Ahh,' Evelyn nodded. 'I've heard my Rockstar has a lovely new friend. So what else has been going on there? I've talked with the new lad Wally quite a bit but old Dick just seems put out that I'm here.'

Alice-Miranda told Miss Pepper all about the first day she and Millie went to visit Wally and how Bonaparte had got loose and charged into the stables. Wally was terrified about riding Rockstar at first but he had done marvellously. Miss Pepper agreed that if she'd been Wally she'd have been petrified too.

'That horse has always been a one-woman animal, I'm afraid,' Evelyn said. 'I'm stunned that the lad has done so well. Sounds like we should keep him for sure.'

'It's wonderful that Rockstar can still run in the Queen's Cup on Sunday,' said Alice-Miranda happily.

'I hope you're right,' Evelyn replied. 'Dick doesn't seem as keen as I'd hoped.'

Mrs Smith returned with two steaming cups of tea and a hot chocolate for Alice-Miranda. She placed Evelyn's on the portable tray and wheeled it in close to her.

'How are you feeling?' she asked her friend.

'I think I might be able to convince the doctor to let me go home for the Cup,' Evelyn replied.

'That's great news,' Alice-Miranda grinned. 'Mr Wigglesworth was very concerned that they'd let you out too early and you'd overdo it.'

'If he's so concerned, he should have come to visit a little more frequently. The lousy so-and-so has only been here twice,' said Evelyn, frowning. 'And he spent the whole time telling me that he didn't think Rockstar should run in the Cup. It was too much of a risk, blah, blah, blah. Anyone would think he didn't want us to win it!'

'I think he's just worried about you, Ev, that's all,' Doreen said. 'You know Dick.' She shrugged.

'That's just it. I thought I did but he's been behaving very strangely since I've been in here.'

'What's that you've been looking at?' Doreen Smith picked up a real estate magazine sitting on the bedside table. 'Are you buying a place?'

'Yes. I think it's high time I had my own little patch of ground. I'm getting too old for this game, Doreen,' Evelyn Pepper declared. 'I've found a lovely holding up north near a village called Penberthy Floss. I want to have a look at it once I'm out of here.'

'That's not far from where I live at Highton Hall. It's the next village along from Highton Mill,' Alice-Miranda said. 'It's so pretty. But it's a long way to drive to work each day.'

'I'm rather hoping to retire,' said Evelyn as she thumbed through the magazine and pointed at the cottage she had been talking about.

'But what about Rockstar?' Alice-Miranda asked.

'He'll be fine,' Evelyn said. 'If he wins on Sunday he'll retire to stud anyway. I think it's time to do some things for me.'

'Of course you should,' Mrs Smith said with a nod.

There was a memory tugging at the corner of Alice-Miranda's mind. 'But Mr Wigglesworth wouldn't know what to do without you, Miss Pepper.'

'Dick Wigglesworth will be fine without me. Besides, all bets are off unless Rockstar can bring home the Cup. It's the last piece of silverware missing from Her Majesty's trophy cabinet and I've promised myself I'll get it for her. If he doesn't win, then I'll give it another year,' Evelyn explained. 'Anyway, I've spoken with Dick and he's going to take Bonaparte to the showground for you in the morning, Alice-Miranda,' Evelyn said.

'Thank you, Ev,' said Mrs Smith. 'I was thinking I'd have to drive Alice-Miranda over to your place before dawn so she could get the pony ready in time and over to the ground.'

'It's the least we can do. I'm sure the only reason Rockstar's not still having a mighty great sulk is because of Bonaparte. And Dick will float Bonaparte back to Chesterfield Downs on Friday evening and have him at the showground again on Saturday. I hope that's all right, Alice-Miranda. I just don't want to risk separating them at this stage. I'm planning to take Bony to the racetrack on Sunday too,' Evelyn explained, 'if that's all right with you?'

'That's perfect, Miss Pepper,' said Alice-Miranda. 'I'm just glad that Bonaparte's being a good friend.'

The trio chatted a while longer before Mrs Smith noticed that it was almost six and said they should be getting back. Alice-Miranda gave Miss Pepper a peck on the cheek. Mrs Smith did too.

'See you on Sunday, Miss Pepper,' Alice-Miranda said with a wave. 'And good luck. I'm sure that Rockstar will do his best.'

'And good luck to you for tomorrow, my dear. Give Bonaparte a special hug from me,' Evelyn replied.

Chapter 29

Thursday night at Grimthorpe House was utter chaos. Several girls were busy ironing their riding shirts, which was no easy task; others were packaging up their cakes and biscuits to take the next day; Ivory was sobbing in the downstairs kitchen because the sponge cake for her lamingtons was as rubbery as a bald tyre and Sloane was busy deciding what dress she'd wear to the ball on Saturday night. She had half of Jacinta's wardrobe strewn over their bedroom floor. As the clock in the hall struck nine Mrs Howard might as well have been herding cats as she tried to get everyone into bed.

Somehow just before ten the house was quiet and the next morning, to Mrs Howard's great surprise, everything ran exactly to schedule.

The showground was a kaleidoscope of colour. In the main arena ponies paraded around the edge of the track, while in the centre a challenging jumps course was proving difficult for even the most seasoned of riders. Millie and Alice-Miranda had competed in two events so far, pairs hacking and showmanship. Unfortunately Bony and Chops decided to have a noisy squabble during the latter, with their bad manners noted by the chief judge.

'I see your little fellow is very poorly behaved, Millicent,' Myrtle Parker commented as she turned and whispered the score to Mrs Howard, who had the unenviable task of following the floral-clad woman around the ground recording the results. She had no idea how she came to be given that particular job.

Howie grimaced and mouthed 'don't worry' to Millie and Alice-Miranda.

'I'm sorry, Millie, that was Bony's fault. Chops has impeccable manners – it's this fellow who needs to behave,' said Alice-Miranda. She glared sternly at Bonaparte. Bonaparte bared his teeth.

'I think our chance of being reserve champions has just floated away on the smell of Mrs Parker's stinky perfume,' Millie sighed.

'Don't worry, Millie. Let's just have some fun.' Alice-Miranda smiled at her friend as the two girls led their ponies over to the temporary stalls for a rest before their next challenge.

Around the edge of the ground, the carnival rides were lurching to life. Noisy music blared from the speakers, frequently drowned out by announcements about the different events. The tantalising smell of barbecued meat mingled with the sweet smell of fried foods and the tang of animal manure. Alice-Miranda had kept an eye open for Fern and Tarquin but they were nowhere to be seen.

Susannah rode past on Buttercup with a beautiful blue ribbon pinned to the pony's bridle.

'Congratulations,' Alice-Miranda called out. 'What did you win?'

'The under-thirteen showjumping,' the girl called back.

'That's fantastic,' Millie grinned. 'That course looked super hard.'

Despite Millie's predictions, by the end of the day she and Alice-Miranda had managed to pick up several rosettes too. Bony and Chops had worked like clockwork in the walking and trotting division. Much to Mrs Parker's obvious distaste she couldn't find fault with their entire routine and had to award them the blue ribbon. There was also a second place in the barrel race and a third for the keyhole, which Mrs Parker thought entirely unsuitable for a genteel country show. Given that the results were deter-mined by the competitors' times, the girls deserved their place fair and square.

At four o'clock all of the horses and riders from Winchesterfield-Downsfordvale gathered together to head back to school. Miss Grimm and Mr Grump stood in front of the group.

'Well done, everyone, you've made me very proud today,' Ophelia Grimm told her young charges as she waved a half-eaten stick of fairy floss like a conduc-tor's baton. A huge smile was plastered across her face. 'Now, you'd better head home, girls, and get a good rest this evening. Tomorrow is another busy day, and then of course the ball is tomorrow night.'

The group began to move off. Some of the girls trotted ahead on their ponies while the rest of the school walked together, chatting about their favourite parts of the day and planning their outfits for the ball.

'Do you want us to wait for you, Alice-Miranda?' Millie called. She and Susannah were sitting astride Chops and Buttercup at the back of the group.

'No, you go ahead, I won't be long. I think that's Wally coming now,' Alice-Miranda called back.

Wally pulled up in the truck from Chesterfield Downs ready to transport Bonaparte back with him.

'Looks like you've had a good day, miss,' he said, admiring the ribbons Alice-Miranda was holding.

'Yes, Bony's done quite well and so has Chops. Millie and I surprised ourselves. But I think we surprised Mrs Parker even more.'

'Well, I'm glad we're taking this one back with us. Rockstar's been making an awful lot of noise today and he was a right monster at the track this morning. I couldn't get him to budge,' Wally complained.

'He wouldn't run?' Alice-Miranda frowned.

'Not a stride. It was all I could do to get him down to the track. I just kept on telling him that Bony would be there. Freddy even went and got one of the other old mares and stood in the distance trying to convince Rockstar it was your little mate, but he's a smart one, that horse. He didn't buy it at all.'

Alice-Miranda shook her head and gave Wally a sympathetic smile. She turned to Bony and began to lead him up the ramp and into the truck. 'You be a good boy, Bonaparte, and have a word to your friend. He doesn't need to be so stubborn.'

Wally took over and tied Bony into the stall. Alice-Miranda planted a kiss on the pony's nose and skipped out of the vehicle.

'Do you need a lift?' Wally asked as he raised the tailgate and locked the back of the truck. 'I've got to go right past the school gate.'

'No, thank you, I think I'll walk. But can you look after these for me?' She handed Wally her bundle of ribbons. 'There's someone I'm hoping to see.'

Alice-Miranda waved as Wally hopped into the truck and turned the key in the ignition. The vehicle clattered into life and surged forward.

The girls had seen Lucas and Sep a couple of times during the day, and the boys had sat with Jacinta and Sloane to watch several of Alice-Miranda and Millie's events. Lucas had won first prize in the art competition for his watercolour and Sep's pipe band had led the morning's parade around the showground.

Fern and Tarquin, on the other hand, seemed to have vanished into thin air since Alice-Miranda last saw them over a week and a half ago. She was hoping that they'd be around somewhere at the showground now. Alice-Miranda walked back through the carnival rides and spotted Ivy bobbing up and down on a cream-coloured pony on her family's carousel. She waved to the young girl, who waved back as she disappeared on another revolution.

The caravans were parked in the paddock beyond the showground. Alice-Miranda decided to go and see if Fern was at home.

As she made her way through the maze of mobile residences, Alice-Miranda heard a gruff voice. She walked a little further between two of the vans, then stopped.

'All right, you lot, listen up. You know the drill. And I'm pleased to say that this little lady has finally decided to join the team. Tomorrow night there's a ball and everyone within twenty miles of this place will be there. Which means that every house and shed and garage within twenty miles will be empty. We've got some very good leads, so, you know what to do.

Head out in pairs, get what you can, don't get caught, and take it all to the barn. And by the way, I want my little gnome friend back again. I miss him.'

Alice-Miranda gasped. She hadn't wanted to believe the gossip, but now she'd heard proof of it with her own ears. And it was up to her to stop them. Alice-Miranda had to find Constable Derby. She spun around and crept back down the narrow gap between the vans. She'd almost reached open ground when she tripped on a rope and fell to her knees.

'Ow!' She clasped her hand over her mouth. But it was too late.

'Oi! What's that?' the gruff voice growled. 'Fern, go and see what that was. And if it's anyone snooping about, bring 'em back here. I've got just the thing for 'em.'

Alice-Miranda scurried to her feet. She turned around and saw Fern's amber eyes glaring at her.

But what happened next took Alice-Miranda completely by surprise. Fern whispered, 'Please just go. Get out of here and don't say a thing. I promise, it's not what you think!'

There was a look of horror on Fern's face. Alice-Miranda didn't know *what* to think.

'Fern, what was it?' the voice growled.

'It was nothing, Alf, just a cat,' she called back.

Alice-Miranda felt as if her lungs were ready to burst as she ran towards the main road. Her mind was racing. Why did Fern let her go? Why didn't she tell Alf? There was more to this – there had to be.

Alice-Miranda jogged down the high street and past Mr Munz's store. The police station was just across from the church. Should she tell Constable Derby what she'd heard? Just as she was about to cross the road, she caught sight of Billy Boots on the other side of the low stone wall. He was standing in the graveyard. Alice-Miranda wondered what he was doing there.

'Mr Boots,' she called, and then walked through the gate and into the church grounds. 'I thought it was you.'

'Oh, hi there,' he replied, sniffing.

Alice-Miranda noticed that his eyes were red and there were streaky marks on his cheeks. 'Are you all right?' She reached out and touched his arm.

'Yeah, of course. Just get choked up sometimes in cemeteries. Thinking about all those people who've died, some of them far too young,' he said quietly.

They were standing in front of the timber cross that Alice-Miranda thought belonged to Fern and Tarquin's mother.

'Where are you heading?' he asked. 'I thought you'd be off home for a rest.'

'I have to find Constable Derby,' Alice-Miranda said. 'I'm afraid that something terrible's going to happen tomorrow night.'

Billy looked at Alice-Miranda closely. 'What do you mean?'

'I should tell Constable Derby, Mr Boots. But let's just say, I think you were right about the carnival people.'

'Why? What do you know?' Billy asked. 'What are they up to?'

'I went to look for Fern and Tarquin, those children I met at Gertrude's Grove a couple of weeks ago, but when I got to the caravans Alf was having a meeting. I couldn't see how many of the kids were there but he was talking about empty houses and good leads. I think they're going to rob the village when everyone's at the ball tomorrow night,' Alice-Miranda explained. 'And worst of all, I think Fern's part of it.'

Billy Boots sighed. He locked his hands on top of his head, then sat down on the edge of a raised gravestone and looked up at Alice-Miranda.

'Sit down,' he instructed, patting the stone beside him.

Alice-Miranda looked into Billy Boots's amber eyes. And right then she knew.

'There's something I have to tell you,' he said, exhaling deeply. 'But you have to promise me you won't breathe a word.'

Chapter 30

Saturday progressed much the same way as the day before. Millie and Alice-Miranda managed to add more ribbons to their haul, winning individual first and second places in the junior showjumping. Millie beamed; she hadn't expected Chops to beat Bonaparte.

'Are you all right?' Millie asked Alice-Miranda when they left the ponies and headed off to get some lunch.

'I'm fine,' Alice-Miranda smiled.

'You seem like you're a million miles away,' Millie said with a worried frown. 'You know I can tell when something's bothering you. And today you're bothered.'

Alice-Miranda shook her head. She hated keeping secrets from Millie. They'd shared so much over the past year that it didn't seem right to keep anything from her. But Mr Boots had begged her not to say a thing.

'Come on, let's go and have a look at this painting of Lucas's. Jacinta said that she wants her mother to buy it for the cottage,' Alice-Miranda said.

Millie giggled. 'Jacinta would ask her mother to buy a paddle-pop stick if she thought Lucas might have eaten the ice-cream off it,' she declared.

Alice-Miranda shuddered, then grinned at her friend. 'That's gross, Millie.'

'But true.' Millie grabbed Alice-Miranda's arm and they headed for the pavilion.

As the girls neared the building, a ruby-coloured Bentley turned into the showground driveway. The flag on the front betrayed its owner's identity.

'Aunty Gee's here.' Alice-Miranda's face lit up and she tugged Millie towards the car.

A smart-suited chauffeur emerged from the

driver's seat and stood sentry at the back passenger door. Aunty Gee's personal bodyguard, Dalton, hopped out of the front passenger seat and ordered away the curious group of onlookers who'd already gathered. Two more vehicles pulled in and a posse of security men alighted and took up their positions around the vehicle.

'You know Mrs Parker will be beside herself,' Millie whispered to Alice-Miranda with a glint in her eye. 'Did she know Aunty Gee was coming?'

'I'm sure it would have been planned,' Alice-Miranda replied. 'You know poor Aunty Gee doesn't get to do anything much on a whim.'

Seconds later, just as Millie had predicted, Myrtle Parker raced out of the pavilion towards the car. She must have been attempting to camouflage herself in the flower exhibition; her dress was bursting with blooms and her purple hat resembled an upturned tulip.

'She'd better not stand still for too long or someone will mistake her for curtains and try to hang her up,' Millie giggled.

Myrtle flounced and preened as she waddled towards the car gripping a large bouquet of roses.

Alice-Miranda and Millie were standing as close to the vehicle as the security men would allow.

Myrtle glared at the pair of them and then sniffed as though she suspected that one of the girls had stepped in something unpleasant.

The chauffeur opened the door and Queen Georgiana stepped out.

'Oh, Your Majesty, it is an honour to see you again.' Myrtle curtsied so low that Millie wondered if one of the security guards would have to lift her back up.

'Hello Mrs Parker, it's lovely to see you again too. I presume the show's going well?' The Queen offered Myrtle her gloved hand. Myrtle momentarily wondered whether she should kiss it or shake it. Fortunately she opted for the latter. Myrtle handed Her Majesty the roses, which Aunty Gee dutifully smelled and then passed to her lady-in-waiting, Mrs Marmalade.

'And *hello* my little lovelies,' Queen Georgiana greeted Alice-Miranda and Millie, who both curtsied too. 'Oh enough of that, haven't you got a hug for your Aunty Gee?'

The girls rushed forward and were enveloped in Her Majesty's ample bosom.

'I was hoping to see you two. I hear that your Bonaparte has become quite the good friend to my

Rockstar,' said Queen Georgina. She stepped back to look at the girls. 'Where is the little man?'

'He's in the stables down near the arena,' Alice-Miranda replied.

'I'd like to pop down and say hello, if I may?' Queen Georgiana asked.

Alice-Miranda took her by the hand. 'Of course, Aunty Gee. Bony would love to see you.'

'And Chops would love to say hello too,' Millie added. The Queen slipped her other hand into Millie's and together the trio began to walk off.

'But Your Majesty, we have tea, in the pavilion,' Myrtle Parker called out. 'And there are people waiting to meet you. It's . . . it's on your schedule.'

Her Majesty turned her head. 'It's all right, Mrs Parker, don't get angsty, dear. I'll be back soon. I'm afraid Bonaparte has performed something of a miracle and I want to thank him. It's because of him that I have a runner in the Cup tomorrow and one who has a jolly good chance of winning the darn thing. I shan't be long.'

Myrtle Parker let out a noise to rival Bonaparte's best whinny. The crowd drew a collective gasp as Myrtle huffed and blew and stormed back inside, shouting at anyone who dared get in her way.

'That Mrs Parker's rather highly strung, isn't she?' Aunty Gee commented on the way to the stables.

'You mean Nosey Parker,' Millie said.

'Millie, that's unkind,' said Alice-Miranda.

'Perhaps, but never a truer word was spoken,' said Aunty Gee. She winked at Millie.

Alice-Miranda changed the subject. 'Are you coming to the ball tonight?'

'I wouldn't miss it, dear. It's always a lot of fun. And I heard that your Miss Grimm has finally seen sense and is letting all of you girls attend too.'

'Yes, but we have to be home by 10 pm, otherwise no one will have the energy for the races tomorrow,' Alice-Miranda informed her.

The group reached the stables.

'Hello there Bonaparte,' said Aunty Gee. She patted the pony's nose and blew softly into his nostrils.

Bonaparte bared his teeth.

'I see you are just as ill-mannered as my Rockstar. It's no wonder you get on so well,' Aunty Gee observed.

Alice-Miranda clucked her tongue at the naughty pony. 'Bonaparte Napoleon Highton-Smith-Kennington-Jones, behave yourself. You are in the presence of the Queen.'

Millie giggled.

Bonaparte lifted his tail and expelled a volume of gas that might have run the school heating for a month.

'You're disgusting,' said Alice-Miranda, cringing. 'I'm so sorry, Aunty Gee. He's not usually this badly behaved.'

'Don't apologise, dear. Rockstar's twice as bad. I've never known a horse to fart as much as he does.'

Millie roared with laughter. She didn't know what was funnier – the image of Rockstar and his wind or the fact that the Queen had just said the word 'fart'. When finally her sides stopped heaving she asked Aunty Gee if she'd like to meet Chops, and assured her that he would be much more respectful than his little friend.

Chapter 31

'My favourite part of the whole night was definitely Mr Plumpton and Miss Reedy doing that ancient Michael Jackson dance,' Jacinta giggled. 'They must have practised for ages.'

'You mean "Thriller",' Millie said.

'I suppose so. Mrs Howard said that she saw them rehearsing in the gym,' Sloane said.

'It *was* pretty cute,' said Millie.

'It was totally embarrassing,' Sloane said with a grimace. 'But it was worth it to see the look on

Mrs Parker's face. She was so annoyed about them stealing her limelight.'

'I think they're gorgeous and I can't wait until they get married,' Alice-Miranda piped up.

'Married!' Jacinta exclaimed. 'Are you serious?'

'Well, it's obvious that they're madly in love,' Alice-Miranda said. 'Perhaps they just need cupid to help things along.'

'Oh no, what are you thinking now?' Millie groaned.

'Your mother seemed to be in good spirits,' Sloane commented to Jacinta.

Jacinta pulled a face. 'Of course she was. Did you see all the attention she was getting from old Hairy Lipp? But at least she didn't abandon me completely – we actually had quite a good talk in the end,' Jacinta admitted.

'Remember when Mr Lipp had a crush on Miss Reedy when we were doing the play with the Fayle boys?' Millie said. 'And that suit he was wearing last night. He must go to the same designer as Mrs Parker.'

'Jacinta and Lucas looked pretty cosy,' Sloane teased.

'He's so handsome,' Jacinta sighed. 'He'd better marry me – or else.'

'Or else what?' Sloane asked.

'I don't know. Isn't that just what you say?' Jacinta shrugged.

'What about Aunty Gee? She was dancing up a storm with Professor Pluss and then even Charlie had a spin around the floor with her,' Millie said.

'She's adorable – and very forgiving. I couldn't believe what Bonaparte did to her this afternoon. He's so naughty,' said Alice-Miranda, blushing at the memory.

Jacinta, Sloane and Millie began to giggle. When Millie had told them all about Bony the windy pony, the three of them had wound up rolling around on the floor holding their sides.

'Oh no you don't,' came Mrs Howard's voice behind the girls. She was patrolling the halls of Grimthorpe House and having a very difficult time convincing any of her charges to hurry and get ready for bed. 'Come along, girls, its way past your bedtime and you have to be up early again tomorrow. I for one am dead on my feet.'

'But it was really funny, Howie,' Millie said, stifling a giggle. 'You wait until I tell you tomorrow. I guarantee your sides will split.'

'All right, you can tell me tomorrow. I need a good laugh after the two days I've had.'

'Goodnight Howie,' said Millie with a yawn as she pushed open her bedroom door.

'Goodnight Mrs Howard.' Alice-Miranda gave her a wave.

Sloane and Jacinta did the same and the girls disappeared into their bedrooms.

Alice-Miranda wondered what was going on out there in the world around her. She was thinking about Fern and Billy and Alf but her eyes were so heavy she could barely keep them open. She climbed into bed and said goodnight to Millie. For the first time in a long time, every girl in the house was sound asleep before the last light was out.

Chapter 32

'Alice-Miranda, wake up.' Mrs Howard gently shook the child. Her eyelids fluttered open and she wondered if she was dreaming. 'Miss Pepper needs to speak with you.'

'Miss Pepper?' Alice-Miranda rolled over and looked at the clock beside her bed. It was just after 7 am.

'It must be important for her to be calling at this hour,' said Mrs Howard as she passed Alice-Miranda her dressing-gown.

The child jammed her feet into her slippers and tiptoed out of the room with Mrs Howard. When they reached the sitting room, Howie passed Alice-Miranda the telephone.

'Hello Miss Pepper,' the girl spoke into the handset. 'What do you mean he's gone?' Alice-Miranda's eyes were now wide open. 'I'll check the stables and call you straight back.'

'Who's gone, dear?' Mrs Howard asked.

'Bonaparte!' Alice-Miranda replied. 'Miss Pepper was allowed to go home from the hospital late yesterday afternoon. After the show Wally took Bonaparte back to Chesterfield Downs and Miss Pepper said that she checked on the horses herself last night. But this morning Bonaparte was gone.'

'You know what a little fiend he is, dear. He's probably just escaped and decided to come home.' Mrs Howard placed her hand reassuringly on Alice-Miranda's shoulder.

'I hope so,' said Alice-Miranda anxiously. 'We have to find him. Rockstar won't run a step without him at the track this afternoon. They've become inseparable.'

Alice-Miranda raced out the back door. In the velvety half-light of morning she could see the outline of several horses in the paddock beside the stables, but none of them looked like Bonaparte.

She entered the building and was greeted by a soft nicker.

'Is that you, Bonaparte?' she called, a warm sense of relief flooding her. But as she got closer she realised that it wasn't Bonaparte at all. It was Susannah's pony, Buttercup. Alice-Miranda ran from stall to stall, hauling herself up to check each one, but Bonaparte was nowhere to be found.

The door to the flat upstairs opened and Billy Boots emerged.

'What are you doing up so early, miss? I'd have thought everyone would be having a sleep-in after last night,' he asked as he bounded down the stairs.

'Bonaparte's gone,' Alice-Miranda said.

'But he never came home. Remember, Wally took him back to Chesterfield Downs.' Billy frowned at her, wondering if she might be sleepwalking.

'I mean he's gone from Chesterfield Downs,' Alice-Miranda said. 'Miss Pepper telephoned just a little while ago. His stall door was open and he was gone.'

Billy gulped. 'Oh.'

'You don't think . . .' Alice-Miranda began.

'It's not likely. It's not his thing, livestock,' said Billy.

'Did you speak to Constable Derby yesterday?' Alice-Miranda asked the lad.

'Yes, he knows what's going on,' Billy said grimly.

She was thinking about Bonaparte and wondering where on earth he could possibly be.

'I need to phone Miss Pepper and let her know that Bony's not here,' Alice-Miranda said. She remembered there was an ancient wall phone in the tack room and immediately went to make the call.

Evelyn Pepper answered and told Alice-Miranda that she had sent all of her lads off in different directions to check that Bonaparte hadn't decided to take a wander around the farm.

'What are you going to do?' Billy asked Alice-Miranda when she hung up the telephone.

'I'll get Millie, and we'll go out on Chops and Stumps to look for the little monster. I know he's clever but I didn't imagine he could open the bolt on his own and escape. That pony!' She shook her head. 'What about you?'

'I'm going down to the station. Constable Derby

should start getting some phone calls this morning. I guess we'll just have to wait until Fern gives us the sign and then Constable Derby can make his move,' Billy explained.

'Well, be careful,' the girl said seriously. 'That Alf's a brute. It sounds like he could be dangerous.'

'I can handle Alf,' said Billy. 'He's not dangerous; he's just a boofhead who thought he could make some extra cash on the side. He didn't expect me to ever stand up to him. We've just got to get the timing right. I can get Chops and old Stumpy ready for you. But you might want to put some proper clothes on.'

Alice-Miranda realised she was still in her gown and slippers. 'Thanks, I'll go and get Millie.' She scurried off to wake her friend.

Chapter 33

Alice-Miranda and Millie had covered miles of ground in their search for Bonaparte. He wasn't anywhere in the school and they'd been down every street and lane in the village too.

'You know, someone might have stolen Bony,' said Millie.

'I'm sure that's not the case,' Alice-Miranda replied.

'I suppose there aren't too many people who could steal the little monster – he's so mean, most thieves wouldn't be able to handle him at all,' Millie began and then, as if a light globe had come on in her head, she gasped. 'Ah! I bet it was Mr Boots. Bony really likes him and, come to think of it, so does Rockstar. I bet that's his plan – that why he's always saying weird things.' Millie decided. 'He's probably going to steal Rockstar too.'

Alice-Miranda shook her head. 'Mr Boots didn't steal Bonaparte.'

'How can you be so sure? You know I've had a strange feeling about him ever since he arrived,' Millie said.

'It wasn't him,' Alice-Miranda replied firmly.

'Well, I think we should tell Constable Derby,' said Millie.

'No, Millie, he didn't take Bony. I'm sure that no one has taken him. He just got out, that's all.'

But Millie wasn't convinced.

As the girls neared the showground, they saw Constable Derby's police car driving slowly through the carnival rides.

'I wonder what he's doing here,' Millie said. 'Let's tell him about Mr Boots.'

'No, Millie, there's nothing to tell. Please trust me,' said Alice-Miranda.

An uncomfortable silence had draped itself over the showground like an unwelcome fog at a summer picnic.

The car approached them slowly. The constable put the window down and greeted the pair. 'Good morning, girls.'

'Good morning,' Millie and Alice-Miranda chorused.

'What brings you out so early this morning?' he asked. He glanced at his watch. It was just past 9.30 am. He'd been up since 5 am himself and hadn't realised where the hours had gone.

'Bonaparte's missing,' said Millie.

'Missing?' the constable quizzed. 'Where was he last night?'

'Chesterfield Downs,' Alice-Miranda replied. 'I think he must have escaped.'

'Really?' The constable sounded cagey.

'I'm sure he wouldn't have been *stolen*.' Alice-Miranda raised her eyebrows at the officer.

Constable Derby twitched.

Millie glanced at Alice-Miranda, wondering why she'd even mentioned the words, given she was so firm a moment ago about Bonaparte having got out.

In the distance the girls could see Mrs Parker's

small hatchback approaching. She was driving all over the road and probably quite a bit faster than she should have been. The car was swallowed by a cloud of dust as she roared up beside the police car and planted her foot on the brakes.

'Constable Derby, Constable Derby,' the woman called. She was near hysterical.

Chops skittered to the left and bumped into Stumps, who whinnied loudly in protest.

'Calm down, Mrs Parker,' said the young constable. He left his vehicle and walked towards her.

'Constable Derby, I've been calling the station since seven o'clock this morning and finally your wife answered the telephone only to tell me that you were out. That's not good enough, young man. I have an emergency.' Myrtle was flapping like a hen in a dirt bath.

'Mrs Parker, I am out on official police business,' the constable replied.

'I don't care if you're out on official royal business, I need to speak with you most urgently,' the old woman insisted.

'What's the matter?' he asked.

'It's Newton, he's gone again,' she sniffed.

'Newton?' The constable's brow furrowed as he struggled to recall why the name was familiar.

'My gnome. He only just came back to me and now the little beggar has disappeared. He was inside the house, too. They've been inside my house!' The woman started to cry and it wasn't long before the sniffle became a wail.

'Is anything else missing?' The constable handed Mrs Parker his handkerchief. She blew into it like a trumpet, then offered it back to him. 'It's all right. You can keep it.'

'I don't know if there's anything else. I just want Newton back,' Mrs Parker sobbed.

Millie was trying hard to smother a smile. She wondered if Newton had packed a bag and called a cab, or perhaps he'd just set off with his suitcase.

'What's the matter with you, Millicent? Do you think this is funny?' Myrtle Parker gulped and sniffed and began to wail again.

Alice-Miranda and Constable Derby exchanged quizzical looks. The police radio in Constable Derby's car crackled.

'Hello darling, it's Louella, can you hear me? Over,' came his wife's voice.

The constable grabbed for the microphone and pressed the button on the side.

'Yes, Mrs Derby, is there something I can help you with? Over,' he answered.

'Oh, you've got someone with you. I'm sorry but you need to get back to the station as soon as possible. I'm afraid there are quite a lot of people who want to talk to you. Over.'

'I'll be there soon. Do you want to take down some details for me? Over,' said the constable.

'I can try but there's a crowd. Over,' Louella Derby replied. It seemed that almost everyone in the village had gathered at the police station. 'And Mr Boots is here. He said that he needs to speak with you most urgently about a barn on the edge of Chesterfield Downs. Over.'

On hearing 'Mr Boots', Millie's eyes had bulged. She opened her mouth to tell Constable Derby her suspicions but Alice-Miranda shook her head and mouthed 'no!'.

'Tell Mr Boots to sit tight and I'll be there in three minutes. Over.' Constable Derby jammed the radio handset back in its holder and jumped into the car. 'Mrs Parker, if you'd like to come to the station later, I'll take down the details,' he called as he turned the key in the ignition and sped off, leaving a trail of dust in his wake.

A barn on the edge of Chesterfield Downs. Alice-Miranda wondered if she and Millie should go there too.

'Isn't that Tarquin?' Millie was pointing towards the caravans.

Alice-Miranda nodded. 'Tarquin,' she shouted and gave Stumps a jab in the ribs. The pony sprang to life and cantered towards the lad. 'Where's Fern?'

'Fern's doing special jobs for Alf,' he said, fiddling with his collection of badges.

Millie gave Chops a kick and cantered over to join her friend.

'Millicent, you come back here,' said Myrtle Parker as she attempted to follow her. 'You owe me an apology, young lady.'

'Let's go, Alice-Miranda,' Millie sighed. 'I'm not apologising to Mrs Parker. I think she's gone crazy.'

'I heard that, Millicent!' The old woman chased after the girls, huffing and blowing like a steam train. She reached the group, took one look at Tarquin and his collection and sucked in a breath so hard Alice-Miranda wondered for a moment if she might choke on it. Mrs Parker pointed at the ground. 'Uh, uh, uh.' She didn't seem able to speak.

'What's the matter, Mrs Parker?' Alice-Miranda leapt down from the saddle and pulled Stumps's reins over his head.

'It was him.' Mrs Parker waggled her fat forefinger at Tarquin.

Alice-Miranda sighed. 'Mrs Parker, I'm sure that Tarquin had nothing to do with the disappearance of your gnome.'

'Then how do you explain that?' she demanded, pointing down among the lad's treasures. 'That is my badge! Mine! He must have taken it from my house when he took Newton.'

Alice-Miranda looked. Millie looked too. A shiny silver badge winked at them in the morning sun. The owner was clear: the badge read *Myrtle Parker Show Society President*.

'Where did you get that?' Myrtle demanded, pointing at the badge.

Tarquin looked up at her. 'Fern got it,' he said.

'Then it must be Fern who broke into my house,' Myrtle raged.

'How long has your badge been missing, Mrs Parker?' asked Alice-Miranda. There had to be a perfectly logical explanation.

'I was wearing it yesterday,' the woman shouted.

Millie tried to recall Mrs Parker and her floral ensemble from the day before. She couldn't remember seeing a badge. 'No, you weren't.'

'Yes, I was. He's a thief,' Myrtle sniffed. 'Anyway, I'm reporting him to Constable Derby. And I'm taking that with me right now.' She reached forward and scooped the badge into her hand.

'No!' Tarquin shouted. 'It's mine!'

The boy reached out and snatched it back again. He placed each badge back into the plastic bag.

'You give that to me now,' Myrtle roared.

'No!' Tarquin lay on top of the bag.

'Mrs Parker, I'm sure that Constable Derby can get your badge back later if it's that important,' Alice-Miranda said calmly.

The old woman stared at the small girl. Myrtle now vaguely recalled that her badge had been missing for weeks.

'Why don't you head home and see Mr Parker,' Alice-Miranda suggested.

Myrtle's face crumpled and she began to cry like a baby. Fat tears ran down her cheeks and she looked completely lost.

'You've had such a busy time. I'm sure that a cup of tea and a lie down would do you the world of good before the races this afternoon. Do you have a lovely outfit? I have a pretty blue dress that Mummy and Daddy sent for my birthday.'

Myrtle Parker nodded.

'Will we see you later?' Alice-Miranda smiled encouragingly at the old woman.

'Bye, Mrs Parker,' Millie said in barely more than a whisper.

Myrtle Parker waddled towards her car, hopped in and drove slowly away.

'Well, that was weird,' Millie said. 'I sort of feel sorry for her. She seemed lost.'

'I think she's exhausted,' Alice-Miranda said, before turning her attention back to Tarquin, who was still lying on the ground guarding his collection. 'It's okay, Tarq, she's gone.'

Tarquin pushed himself to his knees.

'Do you know where Alf is?' Alice-Miranda asked.

'He's gone to the shop,' Tarquin replied.

Alice-Miranda wrinkled her nose. It was Sunday. None of the village shops were open on a Sunday. 'Which shop?'

'The special shop. Near the cats,' Tarquin said, as he pulled his badges back out of the bag and placed them methodically one after the other on the ground.

'Cats? What cats?' Alice-Miranda's mind was in overdrive.

'Miss Bah,' he said.

And then she knew.

'Millie, we have to go.' Alice-Miranda heaved herself up onto Stumps's back.

'Go where?' her friend asked as she wheeled Chops around.

'I'll tell you on the way,' Alice-Miranda called as she took off. 'Goodbye Tarquin!'

Millie gave Chops a sharp jab with her boot and followed after her friend. The two ponies were neck and neck as they raced around the edge of the showground and into the paddock beyond.

'Where are we going?' Millie shouted.

'The stables at Caledonia Manor,' Alice-Miranda called back. 'Just follow me.'

The ponies thundered through the forest. Many hours spent exploring meant Alice-Miranda knew every track and lane. Dodging overhanging branches and clearing fallen logs, old Stumps set a cracking pace with Chops hot on his heels. They raced on until they neared the old vegetable patch at Caledonia Manor and Alice-Miranda steadied Stumps to a trot, then slowed to a walk.

Her heart was hammering inside her chest and she needed to catch her breath.

'What's going on?' Millie panted.

'It's a long story and we don't have much time. I need you to go to Miss Hephzibah's and call Constable Derby. Tell him to get over to the stables here as fast as he can. Mr Boots has got it wrong. It's not Chesterfield Downs – it's here. I'll watch and make sure that Alf doesn't leave.'

'Alf? What's he done?' Millie asked.

'I suspect he robbed half the village last night.'

'See, I told you the carnies weren't to be trusted,' Millie said smugly.

'It's not like that at all, Millie. Do you remember when we first met the kids and there was the fight and Rory said that Alf was coming? They all disappeared. Alf threatens them. He says that if they don't do what he says, their parents will die, just like Gina, Fern's mother, did.'

'That's terrible. Do you think he killed Gina?' Millie asked.

'No, she was sick, but Alf's a powerful man. He can tell the kids what he wants and they're not going to question him. Besides, he already got rid of one of the boys.'

'Who?' Millie frowned.

'Mr Boots,' Alice-Miranda said.

'Billy Boots! What's he got to do with the carnival?' Millie asked.

'Billy is Fern and Tarquin's brother,' Alice-Miranda replied, 'and by rights the carnival now belongs to him and his brother and sister.'

'What?' Millie was shocked.

'Think about it, Millie. What colour are his eyes?' Alice-Miranda asked.

'They're that weird amber cat colour. *Oh*,' she said, nodding. 'Just like Fern and Tarquin.'

'Alf married their mother and then she died and the carnival was meant to be in trust for them until Billy was old enough to take over. But he knew what Alf was up to – except that Alf blamed Billy for being a thief. He accused Billy of stealing the takings from one of their show weekends. He even had photographs which Billy said were completely set up. But the others all took Alf's side, so Billy ran away and he's been working out how to get back there and make things right ever since.'

'That's terrible,' Millie said. 'Poor Fern.'

'We need to get moving. Constable Derby has to catch Alf with the goods, otherwise there's no way to prove it was him.' Alice-Miranda jumped down from Stumps's back and pulled the reins over his head. 'You go to the manor. I'll tie Stumps up here and head down to the stables.'

'Be careful,' Millie said. 'Don't do anything crazy, okay?'

Alice-Miranda smiled. 'I promise.'

Chapter 34

'Miss Hephzibah,' Millie called as she raced along the veranda. She'd hitched Chops to the colonnade on the lower lawn and bolted to the house.

'I'm in here, dear,' Hephzibah called.

Millie flung open the screen door.

'Well, good morning. I was just making some tea.' Hephzibah, in her dressing-gown and slippers, was filling the kettle at the sink. 'You're out early,' she said, glancing at the clock. 'Actually, perhaps we've had a bit of a late start. That ball last night really took it out of me.' It was now almost half past ten.

'Miss Hephzibah, I need to use the telephone, please,' Millie explained. 'It's important.'

'Of course, dear. Is everything all right?'

'I need to call Constable Derby.' Millie ran to the telephone in the hall just beyond the kitchen.

'Constable Derby!' Hephzibah repeated, following Millie. 'Whatever's the matter?'

Millie rang through to the police station.

'Come on, come on, pick up,' she whispered into the receiver. 'Oh hello, Mrs Derby, it's Millie, is Constable Derby there? I need you to get a message to him right away . . .'

Alice-Miranda crept along the fence line towards the decrepit stable block, ducked through the mouldy brick archway and tried to make herself invisible against a stone wall. She watched the entrance of the building for a couple of minutes but all was quiet. Just as she was about to make her way across the open courtyard, she heard the rattling drone of an engine approaching. Alice-Miranda peeked around the wall and saw a battered grey Land Rover turn into the driveway and head straight for the stables. She slipped between the rails and crouched down behind an old stone water trough. The four-wheel drive clattered to a halt in front of the building.

Alice-Miranda peered around the edge of the trough. Someone got out of the car but from her hiding spot she could see only their trousered legs.

'So, my little lovelies, what treasures did you find for Alfie last night?' he said to himself.

Alice-Miranda listened to Alf's footsteps on the cobbles. The stable door groaned as he pulled it open and then closed it behind him.

Alice-Miranda hoped Constable Derby would be along soon. She wondered how she was going to keep Alf there if he decided to leave. Then she had an idea. She slipped back through the fence and scurried across the courtyard to the car. She pulled herself up on the door handle and saw exactly what she was hoping for. The driver's window was down and the key was still in the ignition. Alice-Miranda reached in and held her breath as she pulled the key from the slot. She jumped back down to the ground as softly as she could and hid the key under the water trough. Then she crept to the doorway and listened.

Through a missing panel in the door, she could see the top of Alf's ginger crop. He was standing in one of the stalls, inspecting the stolen merchandise and commenting on each new discovery.

'That's a spanking set of power tools. Yes, I do like a little haul of electrical goods. Mmm, what's this then, jewellery? Lovely. You'll bring a pretty penny down the pub. And my little gnome friend – so glad you're back, son. We can have some lovely adventures this year, and keep your old mum guessing all over again.'

Alf walked out of the stall and further into the building. 'What's this!' he exclaimed.

An explosive whinny punctured the air and Alice-Miranda fell backwards. She scrambled back to her feet, hoping the sound of the pony had masked her tripping on the cobbles.

She knew that voice. It was Bonaparte for sure.

'Feisty little one, aren't you? Well, I'll have to find a new market but you'll bring a pretty penny.'

Alice-Miranda heard the rustle of cloth, then the sound of a pony's teeth snapping.

'Ow! You little monster. I'll teach you to bite old Alfie!'

Alice-Miranda heard some shuffling, then the sound of a horse whip split the air.

'No!' She squeezed through the broken panel and ran towards Alf. 'Don't hurt him!' she yelled.

On hearing his mistress's voice, Bonaparte reared up and smashed his front legs through the rotten stall door, which disintegrated under his weight.

Alf turned to face the tiny intruder.

'What are you doing here, you little snoop?' he roared. 'I'll give you a walloping as well.'

Alf charged forward and slashed at the child with the whip. *Voomp, voomp,* it cut through the stale air.

'Bonaparte!' Alice-Miranda yelled. The pony burst out of the stall and charged at Alf, sending the old man flying. Alf didn't know what hit him as he thudded onto the cobblestone floor.

'Why, you . . .' Alf pushed himself back to his feet. Bonaparte spun around and ran towards the man, rearing up, his forelegs punching forward like a boxer's arms. Alf took several steps backwards. He was cornered in the old feed room. The enormous timber hoppers sat open, their oats and barley mostly gone. Beside them a huge vat of molasses contained a treasure trove of fossilised bugs.

Alf stood his ground but Bonaparte could sense victory. As the ginger-bearded man struck out for the last time, Bonaparte surged forward. With arms rotating like windmills, Alf lost his balance and fell backwards into the sticky trap.

'Ahhh!' he yelled. 'Get me out of here.' But he was stuck fast, the ancient molasses clawing at his backside, dragging his bare arms down into its gummy clutches.

Outside, a police siren wailed. Alice-Miranda heard the car screech to a halt and within seconds Constable Derby, Billy Boots and Fern were inside the building.

'Alice-Miranda!' Constable Derby called.

'I'm here!' She stood up and the policeman rushed towards her with Billy and Fern close behind.

Fern raced forward and hugged Alice-Miranda. 'I'm so sorry. I didn't mean for you to get caught up in all of this.'

'Are you all right?' Alice-Miranda asked. She noticed that the bandage was gone from Fern's arm.

'I'm fine. It's better. I wanted to tell you what was going on the other day when I saw you at the caravans but I couldn't.' Fern's eyes filled with tears. 'It was too dangerous.'

Alice-Miranda smiled at her friend. 'It's all right.

Billy explained everything. It sounds like you've been living with a monster.'

'Who's Billy?' Fern asked.

'Your brother,' Alice-Miranda replied.

'His name's not Billy. It's Liam,' said Fern, confused. Alice-Miranda was too.

'I'll explain later. Where's Alf?' Billy asked, his amber eyes shining in the half-light.

Alice-Miranda pointed at the feed room. 'He's in there.'

Billy and the constable skittered to the door and poked their heads inside.

'What's all this?' Constable Derby exclaimed.

Alf was wedged in the old drum, wriggling and squirming and slowly sinking further into the tacky goo. Bonaparte was standing over him, jabbing his nose into the old man's belly and pushing him further down.

'Got yourself into a bit of a sticky situation there, Alf,' Billy chortled.

'You'll keep,' Alf griped. 'Just get me out of here.'

'Must have something to do with your sticky fingers,' Constable Derby couldn't help but chime in.

He and Billy laughed.

Billy turned and grinned at Alice-Miranda. 'You're a hero, miss.'

The child shook her head. 'Not me. It was all Bonaparte's doing. He's the one you should thank.'

'But how?' Constable Derby looked at the broken timber on the floor.

'Bonaparte caught him.' Alice-Miranda grabbed an ancient lead rope from a hook on the wall and clipped it on Bony's halter. Then she wrapped her arms around the pony's neck and gave him a tight squeeze. 'He broke down the door and didn't stop until Mr Alf was well and truly stuck. The stolen goods are in there.' Alice-Miranda pointed at the end stall.

'But what was Bonaparte doing here in the first place?' Constable Derby asked. 'Did they steal him too?'

'I don't know. But I'm glad that he was.' Alice-Miranda glanced at her watch. 'Oh no! I've got to get him to the racetrack. The Queen's Cup starts soon.'

The sound of hooves on cobbles signified the arrival of Millie and Chops. The girl abandoned the pony and raced inside.

'I heard the siren,' she puffed. 'Huh? What's Bony doing here?'

Alice-Miranda shrugged. 'I don't know but I have to get him to the racetrack or Rockstar doesn't stand a chance.'

'You'd better get going then,' said Fern.

'Don't worry about old Alf here. We'll take care of him. Just go,' Constable Derby commanded.

'Come on,' Millie said. 'Bony's not saddled up, so you'd better double on Chops with me and hold Bony's lead. We should be able to make it.'

Alice-Miranda ran Bonaparte down the centre of the stables. She turned and looked at Constable Derby. 'Oh, if you're looking for the key to Alf's car, it's under the trough,' she said.

Millie leapt onto Chops's back and hauled Alice-Miranda up behind her.

'It's going to be a bumpy ride,' Millie told her friend. 'Hang on. Come on, Chops, let's go!'

Chapter 35

Evelyn Pepper had put off loading Rockstar onto the truck until as late as she possibly could. She'd been trying to calm the cranky beast for hours but no amount of brushing and stroking and blowing in his nostrils seemed to work. He was in a right foul mood. She'd been woken around half past four that morning with her champion whinnying at the top of his lungs. When she hobbled to the stables, she discovered the reason for his bellowing. Bonaparte was gone.

At least Wally Whitstable could manage the giant for her – he wasn't afraid of Rockstar, which in itself was half the battle. Although the horse had always been gentle with Evelyn, she was apprehensive about him lashing out, particularly given her mending hip.

Dick Wigglesworth on the other hand had been nothing but a nuisance all morning.

'I think you should call Her Majesty and let her know that he's not running,' the old man suggested.

'Of course he's running,' Evelyn replied. 'We've just got to get him on the truck and to the track. Bonaparte will turn up. I'm sure of it.'

The colour seemed to drain from Dick's ruddy face. 'How *can* you be sure?' he asked. 'There's always next year, you know.'

'But I want him to run today,' Evelyn said firmly. 'Wally's been doing a fantastic job with his training. No thanks to you, I hear. Come on, Wally, if Dick won't help then I know you will. We need to get him loaded.'

Freddy backed the truck up outside and Wally led Rockstar to the ramp.

'He's not usually a bad floater,' said Evelyn. She limped along to the end of the stables, eager to see her boy safely on board.

'Come on, Rockstar,' Wally whispered. 'Up we go.'

The lad jogged alongside the thoroughbred to the bottom of the ramp. Rockstar took three steps up; he looked like he was going to get there, then stopped and refused to budge.

Wally tried again. Rockstar stopped again.

'Miss Pepper, do you remember when he was just a young fella we used to have the radio on in the truck and he seemed to like the music,' Freddy suggested.

'Oh, you're right, Freddy, and it was always loud rock music. In fact, that was how Her Majesty decided on his name – he was nodding his head in time with the strains of some rock star and Her Majesty thought it was perfect for him. I'd forgotten about that,' said Evelyn, smiling at the lad. 'Go on, then, crank up the radio.'

It was certainly unconventional but worth a try.

Dick Wigglesworth objected. 'You'll upset the rest of the stable.'

'I don't care at the moment, Dick. If playing some loud music means Rockstar gets on board that truck then that's exactly what I'm going to do.'

Evelyn wondered if the Dick Wigglesworth she knew had recently been abducted by aliens. Because this one was a right pain in the neck.

Freddy flicked on the radio. Thumping bass blared out.

'Okay, Wally, try again,' Evelyn said as the lad led Rockstar around in a circle. The stallion was pumping his head up and down and he was dancing all over the place.

'Look at him. I think he likes it.' Freddy had a grin as wide as his whole face.

Dick Wigglesworth had disappeared.

'Come on, Wally, let's get him up there,' Evelyn urged.

Rockstar stepped left, then right, he spun around and then like a flash he scooted up the ramp and into the truck.

'Good boy,' Evelyn cooed.

Wally gave him a pat. Rockstar turned his head and bared his teeth.

'Oh, I know who you learned that from,' Wally smiled at the horse. 'She'll find him, don't you worry.'

★

Chops cantered along, with Alice-Miranda clinging with one hand to Millie's middle and holding Bonaparte's lead rope behind her. 'We'll come back for you, Stumps,' Alice-Miranda called as they raced past the old boy. They took every shortcut to the village they knew.

The whole community had turned out for the Queen's Cup. Ladies wore their finest hats and gentlemen their smartest suits. No one was going to miss the social event of the year, in spite of the raft of robberies the evening before. It was all anyone was talking about. Miss Grimm and Mr Grump and the girls and staff from Winchester-field-Downsfordvale were all there, completely oblivious to Alice-Miranda and Millie's adventure. Jacinta and Sloane were sitting in the grandstand with Lucas and Sep, wondering why Alice-Miranda and Millie were taking so long to join them. After Alice-Miranda had raced off that morning, Mr Boots had told Mrs Howard the whole story and they agreed that it might do more harm than good to make a fuss if Bonaparte's disappearance was tied up with Alf and the robberies. As far as Miss Grimm understood, Alice-Miranda and Millie had gone to Chesterfield Downs to help Bonaparte get ready for the day. Mrs Howard had been relieved to take a call from Hephzibah Fayle letting her know that the culprit had been found, Bonaparte was safe and Alice-Miranda and Millie were on their way.

Evelyn Pepper was making her way from the mounting yard to the small grandstand. She knew Her Majesty would be disappointed that they had no hope of winning. In spite of getting safely to the track, Rockstar was now being more difficult than ever, having taken a chunk out of Wally's arm and given his jockey Diego Dominguez a nasty kick on the backside. Worse than that, he seemed to have lost any spark and was now behaving more like a cranky old mule than a champion thoroughbred. Evelyn hardly dared hope that he would run. Aunty Gee was watching her champion through a pair of binoculars. Dick Wigglesworth was standing beside her, and seemed to be in a bit of a sulk.

Evelyn Pepper took her place beside the Queen.

'Are you all right, Evelyn?' Her Majesty asked.

The woman nodded. Her hip was throbbing and she felt as if her head could explode but at least she was here and so was Rockstar.

'Don't overdo it, dear. I'd hate for you to end up back in that wretched hospital.' Aunty Gee picked up her binoculars and scanned the track. 'Can you see what that is?' She passed the binoculars to Evelyn.

'Oh my goodness, is it really?' she gasped.

★

As the girls emerged from the woods on the far side of the racetrack, Alice-Miranda could see the horses jogging towards the barrier. She leapt down from Chops's back, and with Bonaparte beside her, ran faster around the edge of the track than she had ever run before.

Miss Grimm, resplendent in a stunning pink suit and a wide-brimmed hat, caught sight of Alice-Miranda and her pony.

'What on earth?' She nudged her husband. 'I thought she would have been here already.'

'Rockstar!' the tiny child yelled. 'Rockstar, Bonaparte's here!'

Bonaparte let out an explosive whinny that silenced the crowd.

Rockstar, who was being most uncooperative for his jockey, stopped in his tracks and refused to enter the barrier for the second time.

He whinnied loudly in reply. Bonaparte called

back again and the two of them echoed one another, each whinny louder than the one before.

Alice-Miranda reached the public area in front of the winning post. Bonaparte hadn't taken his eyes off the start line on the other side of the track. The whole crowd was staring at her and the black pony.

'Whatever is that child up to now?' Myrtle Parker frowned. She'd had a lie down and was feeling much better. In fact, her spirits had soared on arriving at the racetrack, where she bumped into Queen Georgiana, who congratulated her on a superb show, and asked if Myrtle would like to join her luncheon party.

Diego leaned forward and whispered into the horse's ear, 'Come on, Rockstar, show us you really are a star.'

The barrier attendant lined Rockstar up for one last attempt at entering the gate before the steward would be compelled to scratch the horse from the race. The stallion danced into the stall and stood impatiently waiting for the bell.

The gates opened and they were off and racing. Rockstar missed the start completely and fell straight to the back of the field.

'Oh dear,' Aunty Gee whispered as she peered through her binoculars. Evelyn Pepper was following Rockstar's every move. His main rival, a grey champion called Postman, had charged into the lead.

'Come on, Rockstar, come on, boy,' Evelyn hissed through gritted teeth.

Dick Wigglesworth was strangely silent as he stood on the other side of Her Majesty.

The crowd screamed as Rockstar began to gain ground. He made a charge around the outside and moved into third place, then up to second. Postman was in his sights. The pair rounded the turn and headed for home neck and neck.

Television cameras tracked their every stride and finally, just a nose in front, Rockstar crossed the finish line.

In the stand, Aunty Gee was leaping about like an excited child on Christmas morning. She caught sight of her lady-in-waiting. Mrs Marmalade was sitting demurely on her seat, her gloved hands folded in her lap and her face like stone.

'Oh for goodness sake, Marmalade, Rockstar's just won the Cup. You are allowed to crack a smile, dear,' Aunty Gee tutted before she leaned over and enveloped Evelyn Pepper. 'Well done, Ev, well done! You've won them all!'

She even gave Dalton a quick squeeze before turning to Dick Wigglesworth, who leaned in and offered a more restrained congratulation.

'Have you been taking lessons from Mrs Marmalade on controlling your enthusiasm?' Aunty Gee demanded of the man.

'No, Your Majesty,' Dick replied.

'Well, you could be a little happier than that,' she suggested.

Dick looked around the Queen at Evelyn. 'I suppose she can retire now.'

'And you can finally ask her to marry you,' Aunty Gee declared and nudged Dick, whose mouth gaped open like a stunned cod's. 'It's about time, don't you think? You've been sweet on one another for years.'

Evelyn Pepper overheard Her Majesty and blushed.

'But,' Queen Georgiana leaned in and whispered, 'I think you owe Evelyn and Alice-Miranda an apology first.'

'What? How? How did you know?' Dick gulped.

'In my experience, Mr Wigglesworth, people do very strange things when they're in love. You're fortunate to be surrounded by such resourceful women. And don't think for a minute that I wouldn't have had you arrested if Rockstar hadn't won that race. I only hope for your sake that Ev's in as forgiving a mood as I am.'

Dick didn't have time to reply as Her Majesty charged off to congratulate her champion.

Rockstar came back to the mounting yard with Diego Dominguez pumping his fist. The crowd cheered even more and Aunty Gee and her entourage made their way towards the dais for the presentation. It was going to be a little strange; she'd never presented herself with a trophy before.

'Alice-Miranda!' Aunty Gee called as the group greeted Rockstar. 'Over here, dear.'

Alice-Miranda led Bonaparte through the crowd and into the mounting yard.

Wally Whitstable had hold of Rockstar and was doing his best to get the beautiful silk winner's rug on the horse's back. As Rockstar caught sight of Bonaparte, the giant stallion spun around and whinnied with all his might. The two friends came face to face and Rockstar reached out and rubbed his neck against Bonaparte's. Bonaparte did the same.

'Well done, boys.' Alice-Miranda gave them each a whacking great kiss on the nose. 'Well done indeed.'

And just in case you're wondering . . .

Alf was taken into police custody where he was charged with all manner of offences, including theft and psychological abuse of children. He had enlisted several of the carnival kids to assist him with his sticky-fingered ways, on the threat that harm would come to their parents if they didn't. He'd never hurt Gina but the other kids didn't know that. Alf was a bully and a liar and when the rest of the carnival adults learned what he'd been up to they were horrified and glad to see the back of him. It seemed he would spend some time in prison, at Her Majesty's pleasure.

Billy Boots returned home to his family and his rightful place as the carnival boss. It turns out that the money Alf accused him of stealing was located under Alf's mattress in the caravan with hardly any missing at all. Billy also reclaimed his real name: Liam Sharlan. The first thing he did was find a new teacher and make sure that his sister and brother and all the other carnival kids kept up their education. Alice-Miranda and Millie tried to convince Fern that she could stay at school with them if she wanted to. They even arranged it with Miss Grimm but Fern decided that, for now, her brothers needed her too much. But she promised that they'd be back again next year and she was looking forward to seeing her friends then.

Dick Wigglesworth confessed to Evelyn Pepper that he had hidden Bonaparte at Caledonia Manor. Evelyn was shocked. She didn't understand at all until he explained that he couldn't bear the thought of her leaving and he knew she was planning to once the Queen's Cup was safely in the trophy cabinet. She was even more surprised when he got down on bended knee and asked her to marry him. Evelyn had hesitated for a moment, wondering if he deserved her after what he'd done, but then to the great delight of everyone in the village and especially Aunty Gee, she said yes. Dick begged Alice-Miranda to forgive him, which of course she did. She reasoned that if he hadn't taken Bony to the stables, Alf might have got away with the robberies – and as Aunty Gee said, people do very strange things when they're in love.

Rockstar's racing career ended. He was now considered one of the most successful horses in history and certainly the best racehorse Aunty Gee had ever had – although she happily admitted that he was the rudest too. Alice-Miranda rode Bona-parte over to visit his friend as often as she could. They were always glad to see each other, and like a couple of old men they whinnied and neighed and nickered for hours.

Ambrosia Headlington-Bear settled into life in the village much more quickly than anyone expected. She even realised that she quite enjoyed gardening. Once she finished her own place she was planning to tackle the weeds across the road – she couldn't bear having to look at Mrs Parker's jungle a moment longer, and perhaps the woman could do with a hand. After all, they were both minus a husband in one way or another. Jacinta visited her mother as often as her training schedule would allow and was fortunate to be at the cottage when the editor from *Gloss and Goss* telephoned to ask if they could do a photographic spread of Ambrosia and her new country life. Her mother was in the garden at the time and, Jacinta had thought, probably wouldn't want to be disturbed. She happened to forget to mention the call.

Newton returned home from his adventure at the Caledonia Manor stables and took his place on the mantelpiece. Myrtle Parker vowed that his travelling days were over but sometimes when she collected the mail, a little part of her missed his postcards.

Alice-Miranda fulfilled her promise to Mrs Parker to read to her husband. She'd decided their first book should be *Matilda* by Roald Dahl. There were plenty of interesting characters in the story and she loved reading it aloud. On her second visit, the tiny child could have sworn the man giggled at one particularly funny scene with Miss Trunchbull, but surely that must have been just her imagination.

Cast of characters

Winchesterfield-Downsfordvale School for Proper Young Ladies staff

Miss Ophelia Grimm	Headmistress
Aldous Grump	Miss Grimm's husband
Mrs Louella Derby	Personal secretary to the headmistress
Miss Livinia Reedy	English teacher
Mr Josiah Plumpton	Science teacher
Howie (Mrs Howard)	Housemistress
Mr Cornelius Trout	Music teacher
Miss Benitha Wall	PE teacher
Cook (Mrs Doreen Smith)	Cook
Charlie Weatherly (Mr Charles)	Gardener
Wally Whitstable	Stablehand
Billy Boots	Stablehand

Students

Alice-Miranda Highton-Smith-Kennington-Jones	
Millicent Jane McLoughlin-McTavish-McNoughton-McGill	Alice-Miranda's best friend and room mate
Jacinta Headlington-Bear	Friend

347

Sloane Sykes	Friend
Madeline Bloom, Susannah Dare, Ashima Divall, Ivory Hicks	Friends
Danika Rigby	Head prefect

Fayle School for Boys students and staff

Professor Wallace Winterbottom	Headmaster
Deidre Winterbottom	Headmaster's wife
Lucas Nixon	Student
Septimus Sykes	Student

Chesterfield Downs staff

Aunty Gee	Owner of the property
Evelyn Pepper	Racehorse trainer and manager
Dick Wigglesworth	Stable foreman
Wally Whitstable	Stablehand
Freddy	Stablehand

Villagers

Herman Munz	Owner of the local shop
Marta Munz	Herman's wife
Otto Munz	Herman's son
Myrtle Parker	Show Society President and village busybody
Reginald Parker	Myrtle's husband
Newton	Garden gnome
Hephzibah Fayle	Friend of Alice-Miranda's and owner of Caledonia Manor
Henrietta Fayle	Sister of Hephzibah and stepgranny of Sloane Sykes
Ambrosia Headlington-Bear	Jacinta's mother

Carnival folk

Alf	Carnival boss
Fern	Alf's stepdaughter
Tarquin	Alf's stepson
Ivy, Little Jimmy, Pete, Robbie, Lola, Rory, Stephen, Indigo, Nick, Ellie	Carnival children
Mr and Mrs Kessler	Carnival workers
Jim Joyce	Carnival worker, Ivy and Little Jimmy's father

About the author

Jacqueline Harvey taught for many years in girls' boarding schools. She is the author of the bestselling Alice-Miranda series and the Clementine Rose series, and was awarded Honour Book in the 2006 Australian CBC Awards for her picture book *The Sound of the Sea*. She now writes full-time and is working on more Alice-Miranda and Clementine Rose adventures.

For more about Jacqueline and Alice-Miranda, go to:

www.jacquelineharvey.com.au

Loved the book?

There's so much more stuff to check out online